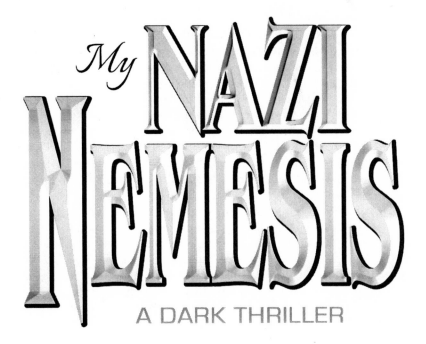

My NAZI NEMESIS

A DARK THRILLER

THE AUTHOR

Rich DiSilvio is an author of both fiction and nonfiction. He has written books, historical articles and commentaries for magazines and online resources. His passion for history, art, music, and architecture has yielded contributions in each discipline in his professional careers.

My Nazi Nemesis is DiSilvio's third novel and fourth book. Rich returns to a WWII setting, which he had treated in his first novel, yet delves deeper into the Holocaust and the depraved nature of human behavior. However, with the protagonist being a cocksure CIA agent with a biting sense of humor and a very colorful supporting cast, the novel emerges out of the darkness to shed humor and light, thus making for an entertaining read.

DiSilvio's previous works include *A Blazing Gilded Age*, which offers a searing look at the ugly underbelly of a golden age, with historical figures, such as J.P. Morgan, Theodore Roosevelt, Mark Twain, Nikola Tesla, and many others woven into the fictional storyline; *Liszt's Dante Symphony*, which is a thriller/mystery, replete with ciphers, spies, serial murders, and a gripping tale that covers the rise of Hitler's Nazi Germany from its Prussian roots under Otto von Bismarck. Finally, there is DiSilvio's magnum opus, *The Winds of Time*, which is a non-fictional tome that astutely analyzes the titans who shaped Western civilization.

DiSilvio's work in the entertainment industry includes projects for historical documentaries, including *Killing Hitler: The True Story of the Valkyrie Plot, The War Zone series,* James Cameron's *The Lost Tomb of Jesus, Return to Kirkuk, Operation Valkyrie,* and cable TV shows and films such as *Tracey Ullman's State of the Union, Celebrity Mole, Monty Python: Almost the Truth,* and many others.

He has written commentaries on the great composers (such as the top-rated Franz Liszt Site), and conceived and designed the Pantheon of Composers porcelain collection for the Metropolitan Opera. The collection retailed throughout the USA and Europe.

His artwork and new media projects have graced the album covers and animated advertisements for numerous super-groups and celebrities, including, Elton John, Pink Floyd, Yes, The Moody Blues, Cher, Madonna, Jay-Z, Willie Nelson, Johnny Cash, Miles Davis, The Rolling Stones, Jethro Tull, Alice Cooper, Eric Clapton and many more.

Rich lives in New York with his wife Eileen and has four children.

My NAZI NEMESIS

Das Lügner

RICH DiSILVIO

Published ℗ 2016 by DV Books of Digital Vista, Inc.
Copyright © 2015 Rich DiSilvio

Printed in the USA. *First printing.*

Cover art and interior book layout by © Rich DiSilvio.
Photographs & images are from purchased collections, photos by the author or courtesy of Wikipedia's public domain images.
Photo of Chevy Bel Air by Kroelleboelle.

ISBN-13: 978-0-9817625-7-9

DV BOOKS
Digital Vista, Inc.
New York, USA

www.richdisilvio.com

CONTENTS

7.   1: Deathfall

12.   2: The First Meeting

17.   3: An American & Soviet in Poland

26.   4: More Wolves

36.   5: Auschwitz

58.   6: Hell on Earth

85.   7: The Visitor

102. 8: Alois Richter

118. 9: Death & Resurrection

129. 10: The Dark Finale

134. 11: The Pangs of Training

143. 12: A Strange Encounter

147. 13: The Assassin

158. 14: Lake Como, Italy

165. 15: A Shocking Honeymoon

187. 16: American Safari

205. 17: Facing the Beast

210. 18: A Boston Tavern

216. 19: The Arch & The Archenemy

230. Photos

232. Real Characters

233. Acknowledgements

1

Deathfall

October 2, 1942

I screamed in bloody terror,

"You sleazy Kraut!" as I was violently shoved out of a Junkers Ju 52 at twenty thousand feet. The herculean thrust of its three mighty propellers blasted me backward, accelerating my unexpected freefall. The airstream tore off my officer's cap and rippled my skin as I fell helplessly through a mist of dark clouds. Perilously, I spiraled toward Earth in the pitch-darkness of night, several miles west of Hamburg, where my body might very well end up mangled and splattered on a dirt road or a small farm in a matter of minutes.

Images of SS *Oberführer* Alois Richter's gloating face flashed before my mind's eye. Just seconds ago, he had stood in the open doorway of the aircraft gazing deep into my panic-stricken eyes while I scratched feverishly to hold onto anything to prevent my fall. By a fluke, I had snatched a parachute mounted near the door just seconds before being maliciously shoved out, yet the dirty pig had drawn his knife and cut a deep gash into the pack's canvas membrane. Just before the dreaded last push, Alois had honored me with one of his sarcastic witticisms as the Kraut cackled, "Well, Jack, look at the bright side. If at first you don't succeed, you'll never jump again!"

Purging the Nazi's nefarious face from my mind, I was now confronted with the grave issue at hand: somehow I had to turn Richter's death-push into a success and prove the bastard wrong.

My hands frantically reached for the parachute's straps, which flapped wildly in the wind, and I began harnessing myself. My heart raced, but nowhere near the dizzying velocity of my decent, which was increasing at an alarming rate. Clothes whistling, my eyes began to water, when suddenly one of the pack's straps whipped around, its buckle carving a crafty gash across my chin.

Once the pack was secured, my fingers quickly began pulling the silk material out of the jagged slit—compliments of the asshole Alois—which I now prayed would catch the wind and deploy with some semblance of a functional canopy.

Gazing upward toward the heavens, I closed my eyes and pulled the ripcord. *Nothing happened!* "God, *no!*" I screamed.

My fingers dug fervently into the slit once more and began pulling out the partially severed silk canopy. Strands of suspension lines began flowing upward, like boiling spaghetti doing a macabre death dance—as if mocking my mortality. Once again, Alois's smug, sinister face appeared before my mind's eye, delighting in his handiwork and the amusing thought of my imminent demise. His illusionary face faded from sight as dark clouds consumed me. Lost in a black void, fear gripped me *tight*.

Turning my gaze earthward, in an attempt to assess how many minutes or seconds I had left to live, I suddenly felt a gut-wrenching jerk as my body bounced upward! As I eagerly gazed skyward, a grunt eked out from the very pit of my stomach. Despite being partially choked by unruly strands of suspension cords, the glorious canopy had miraculously prevailed. It was a sight to behold as purple shades of moonlight cascaded over its soft, silky skin.

Down below I could see faint silhouettes of treetops lining a roadway and an open field near what I suspected was the Elbe River. Pulling hard right on the suspension lines, I attempted to steer myself towards the field. My descent was so rapid I didn't have time to maneuver fast enough, and I crashed into a towering sycamore maple tree, my body sliding down, hitting branch after branch as the soft leaves brushed against my body and brought me to a most welcome stop. Dangling some eight feet off the ground, I quizzically looked upward to find the source of my levitation. There, before my eyes, was a hefty branch gracefully clutching my canopy as if the hand of God. Overwhelmed with bliss, I cried.

St. Louis, Missouri
September 20, 1957

Some people say I have the gift of gab, but actually, I'm a rather private and reserved man. I have to be, being that I was an OSS officer during the war and rolled right into the CIA afterward, when it changed its name.

My name had also changed from Jack Goodwin to Jack Hornsby—for covert reasons—but for clarity in my storytelling I'll use my birth name: Goodwin. I'm Irish-American, but the real deal being born in Cork, Ireland and then transplanted to Astoria, Queens when I was nine. My brownish-red hair and ruddy, white complexion are complimented by hazel eyes, which hover about five feet five inches above the ground. Adding my forehead, I max out at five feet ten inches tall—a little less after I get a crew cut. Well, as I like to say: the Devil Dog is in the details. So I salivate over facts.

Anyhow, my fifteen-year-old daughter Eleanor loves when I reminisce about my escapades in the war. She's a pretty gal with dark brown hair, blue eyes, olive complexion, and is comfortable either reading Jane Austen with a cup of tea or blazing down the track like Roger Bannister. And although she's heard that particular tale of mine several times before, naturally there are many other stories that I felt were too graphic and disturbing to thrust upon her tender little ears. But now that she's a cool-cat teenager in this crazy new world of Elvis Presley's rowdy rock 'n' roll, and Allen Ginsberg's radical Beat Generation I suppose I should be more *hip*.

Gazing over at my daughter, who is currently sitting on the living room couch, chewing on an Atomic Fireball, I'm now prepared to start unlocking the WW II vault buried deep in the back of my thick skull.

"Hey, Daddio, although I've heard that one before, you didn't quite tell it the same way. There are more details and even some nasty words, which you always scold *me* for saying."

"That's true, Ellie. But you're only one year away from your sweet sixteen, and it's time for me to start revealing more information. There are some very important and disturbing things that happened in the past that you need to know."

Eleanor squinted, eyeing me up as the wheels in her sharp little mind turned like a fine Swiss watch. Although Eleanor tried to fit in with her young, rebellious crowd, she was truly a fifty-year-old woman in a fifteen-year-old's body. Pensively, she rubbed her chin. "Well, I've long suspected that this Alois Richter character had more to do with your life than just that deadly skirmish over Hamburg."

Grasping my freshly brewed cup of Joe off my green, Formica kitchen counter, which divides both rooms, I strolled into the living room and took a seat next to her. "You're a very perceptive girl, Ellie. Yes, there's a far greater story to be told. But not just about Alois. Your mother is part of this convoluted equation also."

Eleanor's adorable face withered, now solemn and pensive. "You told me Mom died in 1945, at the end of the war, but never told me how."

"Exactly, princess. And now that you're old enough, I have to get this burden off my chest and enlighten you to the truth. But be prepared, some of this is going to be very ugly. Wartime brings out the worst in people."

My inquisitive daughter fell silent. I could see the anticipation and anxiety consuming her. I swallowed hard, knowing this wasn't going to be easy. But this day had finally arrived, and like a good soldier and special agent, I'm well accustomed to executing tough missions. I pulled out a Camel and my trusty Zippo and lit up.

"Ellie, I think it's best that I start from the very beginning...how I met your mother, and then how Alois entered our lives. Alois's name, by the way, is derived from Latin *Aloisius*, meaning 'famous warrior.' And a bloody warrior he was. Perhaps infamous would be more apropos. Alois also happened to be the name of Adolf Hitler's drunken and abusive father. That should give you a good idea as to how wicked Alois the Nazi Warrior is. He has been my Nazi nemesis for fifteen years."

Eleanor squinted at that last bit of information as she leaned back into the couch and clutched each of her elbows, bracing herself for the coming storm.

2
First Meeting

March 9, 1942

To begin with let me clarify my agency's founding and subsequent name changes. In 1941, America was already involved in world affairs with FDR's cunning Lend Lease program and being hailed as the Arsenal of Democracy. Meanwhile, Hitler's theater of war was expanding rapidly with his *Blitzkrieg*, or lightning war. President Roosevelt was wise enough to realize that we needed a secret service, and in July of 1941 he called upon William "Wild Bill" Donovan to create what would be called the office of the Coordinator of Information, or COI. By June 13, of the following year, its scope broadened and it became the Office of Strategic Services, or OSS, which Donovan was to model after Britain's MI6 with their guidance. Our function, naturally, was to engage in espionage, propaganda, subversion, and sabotage—all devious things that stir my soul with delight.

On March 9, 1942, my mission was to fly a sortie into Poland, parachute out with four other agents—each of us wearing civilian three-piece suits—then make a rendezvous in Munich, Germany by any means possible. The main op would then commence from there. That night we took off from London, the sky was a deep, phthalo blue and fairly clear. Yet upon entering Polish airspace, we encountered dense clouds making navigation difficult. Unexpectedly, anti-aircraft fire shot up like a swarm of colossal fireflies, illuminating the sky—then all hell broke loose!

Our B-24 Liberator hummed and vibrated while our gunners' eyes anxiously scanned the exploding sky for enemy aircraft. Through the mist a Junkers Ju 87 emerged, heading straight for our port side, when Harry Lewis, our ace gunner, yelled, "Jerry at 9:45!" Quickly swiveling about, he emptied several rounds into the dive-bomber's fuselage. Bullet holes speckled its aluminum skin when the Plexiglas canopy suddenly shattered, most likely killing the pilot, who'd lost control. As he careened under us, the top of his rudder blade came ripping through our underbelly, looking like a shark's dorsal fin slicing through metal. Air began gushing in as we all scattered to put on our parachutes. Then the death knell came: a Messerschmitt Bf 110 appeared out of nowhere! It was cruising at over 500 mph with its twin 20mm cannons blaring! Pivoting quickly, I saw the nose of our B-24 being shred into confetti as our pilot and navigator screamed, disintegrating into a bloody mixture of glass, aluminum, and guts.

My wide eyes gazed around to see who else was alive while I swiftly buckled up my harness. Only Harry and I were left standing when the plane began listing into a steep nosedive. Flashing our thumbs-up, we both sought an exit. The fuselage was riddled with large gaping holes, offering us several exits, yet all had sharp jagged edges. Harry was on the opposite side of the aircraft, when I saw him salute farewell. With fear in his eyes, he turned and bailed out. Quickly, I pivoted to face the large breach before me while my body wavered in the blustering airstream. My mind flashed with the thought of how, in a matter of seconds, our quiet flight had turned into a hellish nightmare—the majority of my crew dead and perhaps me too, in a matter of seconds. Making the sign of the Cross, I held my breath and leapt through the opening, out into the unknown.

The vision before me now was surreal. Just darkness and thick layers of clouds, nothing tangible was in sight. I suddenly began choking as the burning smoke trail of our plane's avgas and hydraulic fluid rose up into my nostrils, stinging my lungs. Reaching for the D-ring, I pulled it hard. The canopy unfurled with a *pop!* and I drifted slowly into a dead sea of fog and soot as the caustic smells of sulfur and oil continued to rankle my lungs. It seemed like an eternity before the clouds began to thin and I saw Poland for the first time. A sprawling terrain of meadows and trees emerged, all bathed in the bluish-gray hues of night.

My feet hit the ground, and I quickly unbuckled my harness. Ditching my parachute into the nearby bushes, I promptly patted the counterfeit civilian papers in my vest pocket, sighing with relief they were still intact. I then gazed around doing a 360-degree sweep. All seemed relatively quiet—almost too quiet. A few small pops of gunfire echoed in the distance, but then stopped. My pulse simmered to a calm and steady beat as I called out for Harry using his code name, Karl, and began walking aimlessly. Having completely lost my bearings, and my compass, I simply chose a direction on gut instinct. I walked for a good twenty minutes, calling out "Karl" into the darkness of night, yet heard no response.

While plowing through the tall grass, I suddenly heard an unnervingly peculiar sound. The irritating hum grew louder and louder, sounding like a gargantuan sewing machine, clanking and thumping. My body began to vibrate as the disquieting clacking noise grew rapidly closer. I swiveled to the sound and was thunderstruck! I hit the dirt as an antiquated Polikarpov Po-2 biplane soared over my head, its wheels only two feet away from leaving skid marks on my head.

The breeze whooshed past, and I sprang up to see the bizarre image of this Soviet jalopy as it crash-landed some 80 yards away. I ran toward the wreckage, hurdling over small bushes and tall grass, while being engulfed in drifting veils of fog. As I approached, I could see the Soviet pilot trying to free himself as the five-cylinder radial engine caught fire, quickly igniting the jalopy's wood and fabric frame. Fire spread rapidly and smoke billowed, yet I could still see the pilot struggling to un-harness himself. Scampering toward what now looked like an emblazoned barn fire as the wood and canvas crackled, I peeled off my jacket and beat back the flames. I made my way to the cockpit and pulled out my knife. Startled, the pilot turned and intuitively reached to stay my hand. I shook my head, pointed to the restraining straps of his harness, and went ahead and severed the Grim Reaper's deadly clutches. The pilot smiled, and leapt out of the flames and into the world of the living.

We both ran several yards away when the plane's fuel tank suddenly exploded, our bodies being blasted to the ground while the plane vanished into a blaze of flames and smoke. Anxiously, we sprang up and gazed into the inferno, amazed to be watching the fire and not burning *in* it. He turned and stared at me through charred round goggles, his entire face and leather cap blackened with soot, and he smiled, his white teeth gleaming like footlights on a vaudeville stage. The happy little fellow then embraced me, and, to my surprise, kissed me on the lips. Startled, I pushed him back, only to see him pull off his leather cap to unfurl her long beautiful hair!

St. Louis, Missouri
September 20, 1957

I glanced at Eleanor with a smile as I extinguished my Camel's smelly butt into the ashtray. "And *that* is how I first met your mother."

With a giggle, she replied, "Your plane crash was terrifying, but this tale about meeting Mom was rather sweet. You had me worried. I thought I'd be hearing a horrifying Hitchcock thriller."

"Darling, this story is far from over. Sit back and relax," I advised as I got up and strolled into the kitchen.

I opened the refrigerator and grasped a Schlitz. They say the Milwaukee brew is now the top contender in sales with my local Anheuser-Bush, but to be honest, neither one floats my boat. I'm a Black Label man myself. But my CIA partner always brings this squirrel piss over. She has horrible taste, except in men. You get the idea.

Just to aggravate myself, I then took a peek out the rear window. Christ, tomorrow's Saturday and I'll have to mow the damn lawn, *again*. I had bought this small, redbrick ranch in Richmond Heights to limit yardwork, but even my Irish luck abandoned me. I don't know whom the imbecile was that came up with the idea of manicured lawns and fancy topiary, but having grown up in rustic Ireland and then Astoria, Queens, I prefer either raw, undisturbed nature or hard cement—preferably the latter. I guess I must thank the Romans for that invention; strong, durable, and maintenance free. But too bad they didn't make it in Kelly green.

Walking back into the living room, I popped the top of my Schlity beer and sat beside Eleanor. "Okay, now where was I? Oh yes, it was a foggy night in Poland."

3

An American &
Soviet in Poland

March 9, 1942

*T*he midnight fog began to lift slightly when, to our surprise, searchlights sliced through the clouds like laser rapiers doing a choreographed duel. Unable to speak Russian, I said in German, "*Folge mir!* (Follow me!)"

Her light blue eyes seemed to glow as they peered into mine. "Do you know where you're going?" she asked in perfect English.

My brow rose with surprise, as I replied in English, "Is my German not good?"

"No, it's perfect. It's just that I saw the B-24 go down, but more importantly, I see the handle of your Colt."

I smiled and drew my jacket over the weapon. "And I see *you* speak English, comrade."

"Yes. As well as German, Polish, French and Italian."

"Damn, you foreigners really tan our American hides in the languages department." My eyes did a 180-degree sweep. "But we best get a move on." I clutched her hand and began running toward the dense forest some 300 yards away. "And, no. I don't have any idea where I'm going," I said, "but we certainly can't stay out here on this open meadow!"

Dashing through the grass we came upon the first row of tall trees, which appeared to be like tall sentinels guarding a magical forest, and we slipped in. At about fifty feet in, we came to a stop and spun around. Out of breath, we held our sides, panting. Peering through the webbed network of branches and twigs, we watched the gigantic spotlights scan the sky, forming luminous rays of Xs and Vs. To our surprise, after several swipes the light show unexpectedly ended. We both sighed with relief as our eyes briefly connected and then gazed back at the partially obscured horizon. The air was still and silent. A faint glow illuminated the open meadow as a sliver of the crescent moon pierced through the undulating clouds, like a scalpel cutting cotton.

I gazed back into my new Soviet comrade's eyes and smiled. After exchanging names, however, I was compelled to ask her a burning question. "What the hell were you thinking flying that old, 1920s heap of trash?"

She smiled. "Believe it or not, these old biplanes are actually proving to be very effective. And not just against the *Luftwaffe*, but also their ground troops."

"How so? By making the Krauts laugh to death?"

Veronika smirked. "No! I'll have you know that the word is out: the Nazis *are* frightened of us."

I laughed. "Oh, come on. Now you're pulling my leg."

"I'd like to pull you hair! You're rather fresh."

I realized I might have overstepped my manners so I slapped on my serious face. "I apologize. Please..." a slight giggle escaped before I could finish "...explain."

Crossing her arms, Veronika heatedly tapped her foot on the ground. "Are you finished being rude?"

My eyes quickly scanned the forest for activity as I replied, "Okay, okay. I'm a fool. There you have it. That was your first taste of a silly twenty-seven-year-old American. Now, please, continue."

With skeptical eyes, she said, "You see, these old biplanes are able to fly in very low, just above the treetops, and are undetected by radar due to their wood and fabric construction. Therefore, we stealthily cruise in and then release two or three bombs, which although not many do terrorize the enemy. It's more psychological intimidation than massive bombing, naturally, but we women are proud to do our part."

"Women!?" I burst out laughing. "Oh, come on! Do you mean to say your entire outfit is comprised of women?"

A smirk once again etched her beautiful face. "You're cruising for a slap! Ally or not."

I covered my unruly mouth and turned away to regain composure, spotting a felled tree that had snapped in half, and realized that could be *me* if I kept it up, as I then gazed back into her beautiful blue eyes.

However, it was clear by the look in those eyes that Veronika was still not too enamored with me, as she said, "This is one area that the Soviets do surpass all other nations. Marina Raskova, a great female pilot, formed Aviation Group 122. In fact, the Amazon warriors of antiquity were also from the Ukraine region. So Soviet women have a long and valiant history, Jack. Meanwhile, you foreign males are all just a bunch of knuckle-dragging Neanderthals. And you should all be clubbed!"

I chuckled. "Well, if we get out of here alive, I would love to go clubbing with you. I know several great night spots in London."

That witticism seemed to work as it managed to crack the Amazon warrior's steely armor. She giggled and shook her head. "I heard about you Americans."

My head recoiled. "What do you mean? Are you insinuating that all American men are Don Juans? Remember, Veronika, *Señor* Don Juan was a Spaniard."

"Don Juan is just a stereotype for most men."

"Well, I'll concede that most men are amorous, but God was the one who injected us with testosterone."

"Oh, so you're blaming God?"

I laughed. "Well, we mortal men didn't inject ourselves with it, did we? So whom else should I blame? And don't forget, it was sexy, naked Eve who made Adam fall from grace."

Veronika smiled and waved her hand dismissively. "Oh, please, let's not get into religion. But I'll agree: some women are just as lustful as men and love chasing after them. Meanwhile, I'm running *away* from men. Evil men, that is."

"What do you mean?" I said, my curiosity piqued.

The lovely Russian took off her jacket and all traces of her Soviet uniform and tossed them away, revealing a fancy white lace blouse with an opulent gold brooch studded with rubies, and a maroon pleated skirt that complimented her curvy hips. "Stalin is a sadistic mass murderer, and this was my last flight for that wretched man and his warped country. I've worn these civilian clothes under my uniform on my last three missions, but didn't have the nerve to escape. Now it seems fate took that dilemma out of my hands and had my plane shot down. It then brought you into my life to pull me out of the flames and escort me to safety."

I nearly choked. "Veronika, I'm no angel of mercy or Saint Christopher. Look around. We're lost in some woods, in God knows where, Poland. To say *safety* is a bit premature." My eyes nervously glanced at the forest's perimeter. "Besides, I happen to have great admiration for Russian culture and an interest in communism. God knows capitalism has failed miserably in America. The Depression has turned our once golden paradise into a sprawling ghetto. Granted, Roosevelt's New Deal has created jobs, but as far as I'm concerned, a state-run enterprise is just a variation of Fascism. So I don't know where America is heading these days."

"From what I've heard, Roosevelt's New Deal is only a temporary system to kick-start your economy. Once it becomes productive, the helpful hands of your government will be withdrawn. Yet, in Russia, the bloody hands of Stalin choke and decimate everything. Even German officers are allowed some degree of freedom to voice their opinions to their superiors. Yet in Russia, no one is allowed to dispute a command by Stalin. I mean *no one.* Even those in the highest ranks never know if they, too, will suddenly be deemed an enemy of the state and put to death or sent to a Gulag for a life of freezing hell. Whole ethnic communities have been uprooted and sent to Siberia. Others abandoned and left to starve, while others are executed en masse. No one knows why. And no one dares to ask. It's a nightmarish world of fear and savage brutality."

I rubbed my chin, dumbfounded. I peered around, making sure the area was still secure, and said, "Veronika, I don't doubt you've heard of horrible crimes and conspiracies being committed, every nation seems to have them, but I truly find it hard to believe. The Russia I grew up learning about, and is now our ally, has many Americans joining the Communist Party back home."

Veronika cackled. "Huh! Americans that join the Communist Party in your country are idle country club chatterers who don't know about the blood and guts that spill in our streets and desecrate Mother Russia."

Just then a rustling sound caught our attention. We both turned toward the sound to see an owl gnawing on a small rodent. Glancing back at one another, I said, "You see, it's an ugly world for *all* life on Earth."

"That it is," she said as her eyes anxiously scanned the forest. "So what should we do now?"

"I suggest we just lie low, right here, until daylight."

Veronika nodded and began scooping up a pile of leaves. Having formed a mattress, she sat down.

I smiled. "That looks comfy, can I join you?"

"Who's asking? Don Juan or Jack Goodwin?"

"Well, as you said, we're one and the same."

She chuckled. "Although you're a bit dense and annoying, there is a special charm about you."

I clutched my heart. "You *slay* me. Now I know the rapture of being impaled by Cupid's sardonic arrow."

She shook her head. "You're an idiot. But you did save my life. So, yes, you may have a seat."

My smile grew into boyish grin, like the one I wore when Darla—a girl I had a crush on in grade school—finally accepted my entreaty after three devastating rebuffs. I sat beside Veronika, trying not to stare too much, but found that my eyes kept getting drawn back to her lovely face, soot-stained and all. Her dark brown hair with blond highlights—or perhaps they were red highlights, I couldn't be sure in the dark—was simply radiant. Or at least as radiant as hair can be at night in a dense forest enshrouded with wispy veils of fog. Then again, that's probably my amorous imagination conjuring up an ideal prototype of womanly beauty, because, as I said, God is the one who made this direct hotline from the crotch to the brain, which seems to short-circuit logic. All I knew is that this woman had some crazy spell over me.

She gazed into the sky and back down at me. "Do you know what the Germans call us women pilots?" I shook my head, as she said, "Night Witches."

I laughed. "I was just thinking about how you have some crazy spell over me."

Veronika smiled. "Well, I'm not into black magic, even if my sooty face says otherwise."

We giggled and stared at each other for what felt like seven dreamy seasons, or seven deadly sins. Whatever it was, it was grand.

The songs of crickets and rustling of leaves in the breeze filled the night air along with the sweet smell of pine, as we both leaned on each other and then slowly backwards against a tree. We gazed through a myriad of branches into space as our eyelids grew heavy. Before long I could feel the weight of Veronika's body pressing against me, warm and limp, as she slipped into a peaceful slumber. Meanwhile, regardless of my exhaustion, I had to stay awake. Someone had to be the sentry, and I happily volunteered. Well, let's just say I was chosen by default.

Straining to stay awake, my mind started to rehash my mission. I wasn't here in Poland for a romantic rendezvous with some unknown Soviet Night Witch. I had an operation to perform, a serious operation no less, and had to start thinking of ways to improvise. My entire crew was killed, or in Harry's case, probably just lost, and everything had to change. A complete revamping of the mission was never rehearsed, never even contemplated. *Shit! What a mess!*

Just then, I heard a slight rustling sound in the bushes. My head spun around gingerly, trying to locate the source while not waking Veronika. My eyes strained to focus in the dark, but all I could see was a gray blurry mass. Then suddenly my heart pounded and face flushed as my eyes finally focused! A pack of four wolves were stealthily creeping toward us, their bone-chilling eyes all aglow, like the eyes of the very Devil himself.

I subtly nudged Veronika and quickly covered her mouth. Her eyes bulged as she shifted upright. I released my hand and she whimpered, "Oh my God!"

In a stupid attempt to allay her fear, I whispered, "If you know of any spells, now's the time to use them."

The sharp elbow into my side seemed to indicate she didn't appreciate my levity.

Meanwhile, the four wolves crept ever closer; step-by-step their paws crackled the dried leaves, sending an unnerving chill down my spine. With each crackle I could almost feel the inevitable crunch of our bones in their powerful jaws. In plain English, I was scared shitless.

Slowly, I reached into my holster and slid out my Colt M1911. The alpha male wolf stepped in front of the betas and turned his massive head toward me. His infernal, marble-like laser eyes seemed to pierce right through my pupils, incinerating my retinas and my nerve. His black rubbery lips rippled and saliva dripped as he now prepared to reveal his large white fangs, the razor-sharp canines that would soon be tearing our flesh apart in a bloody frenzy.

Veronika squeezed my left arm tighter as I now pointed the barrel of my gun at this devil in wolf's clothing. I grit my teeth and belched out a menacing growl, thus triggering the mighty alpha's lethal response. With a chilling growl, the wolf lunged toward me! In an instant, his huge head was within ten feet, and that's when I unleashed my .45 caliber chunk of human ingenuity. His head exploded as his massive body skidded into my lap. Veronika screamed while I grabbed the bloody carcass and brandished my trophy. With a primal yell, revealing my own choppers, I showed his beta bitches that this animal takes no prisoners!

St. Louis, Missouri
September 20, 1957

"Dear God!" Eleanor screeched. "That was terrifying."

"Indeed it was."

"But do you mean to say that you always faced danger with a corny joke or two?"

I chuckled as I pushed my half-full can of Shlity squirrel piss away. "Well, I do feel that levity keeps you more relaxed and thinking clearly, because if you let panic reign, it clouds your judgment and could cost you your life. In my line of work it's crucial to outthink your rival. However, I must admit, retelling an event does lend itself to embellishments. For the art of storytelling is likewise an important survival skill." With a wink, I got up to make myself a Tom Collins.

"Hmm, hitting the hard stuff already?" Eleanor commented.

I smiled as I returned to the sofa and placed my highball on a St. Louis Cardinals coaster. Using a Bachman pretzel rod, I stirred my drink and then licked the moist, salty end of my pseudo cigar. "Well, the story will start getting even darker, so a stiff drink will make it a little easier to tell."

Eleanor's cute face suddenly lit up with a sly smile. "So, Daddio, can I have one too?"

I chuckled. "Sure."

Eleanor's eyes widened with delight. "Really?"

"Yes, when you're eighteen." Eleanor smirked as I took a sip and added, "Now let's continue."

4

More Wolves

March 9, 1942

*H*aving eliminated one terror, however, just opened the door for another. No sooner had my shot echoed in the night and the remaining wolves retreated, when a pack of Nazi wolves bore down on us.

My pants were splattered with blood, and as I pushed the gooey carcass away, a patrol of Germans came from all directions, some with flashlights creeping through the woods, while others were being dragged by Alsatians, my dead alpha friend's domestic cousins. Veronika looked at me, but I shook my head. "This doesn't look good. We're surrounded, and I only have one pistol. We can try to make a break for it, but they have German Shepherds, and we can't outrun *them*. Speak German from here on."

As she nodded, I suggested that she hide her expensive brooch as wartime breeds not only killers but also thieves, even of nice people. She complied and buried it in her cleavage. I was a little peeved, hoping she would have asked me to do that since she *did* say her life was in *my hands*, but there were other things that needed my attention right now.

Within minutes the lights were glaring in our eyes as the harsh foreign sound of the German language drilled home the fact that we weren't in Kansas anymore. I discreetly tossed my American-made Colt into the bushes as they closed in on us, pointing their rifles (mounted with razor-sharp bayonets) and restraining their canine chewing machines. I then crossed my arms casually, like a good German would.

Pushing his way to the fore, a tall Aryan wolf, wearing the insignia of a *SS Scharführer,* pulled out his Luger and barked a command to his troops in guttural German, "Stand firm!" Then gazing at us, he barked in English "Ah! Could this be the Night Witch and B-24 American we've been searching for all night?"

"No," I retorted, "I'm Hansel and she's Gretel."

The *Scharführer* snarled at my jest, and resorted back to speaking German, despite not buying my Aryan impersonation. "So, you think you're a comedian, like your foolish American movie stars, is that it, Mr. Costello?"

"Well, you're no bud, Abbot."

It was clear my wordplay went over wolfman's head as his pinched furry brows and wrinkled snout indicated. Regaining his initial charge, he spat, "You will not think it's so funny when I toss both of your asses into my special chamber for questioning!" Turning to his underlings, he waved for them to seize us. With an obedient salute, two young guards approached us and bound our wrists to each other, my right to Veronika's left.

My nostrils flared as I growled, "You'll regret this!"

Wolfman merely chuckled as he pompously gazed at my civilian clothes. "That I doubt. And where did you buy that nice suit? It does look rather expensive."

"Wertheim's on *Leipziger Platz* in Berlin. Why?"

"Ha! I should have guessed. A Jew establishment that *Herr* Wertheim tried desperately to save by making his

Aryan wife Ursula the principle shareholder, but failed. It was taken over by the government and properly Aryanized. It is now called AWAG. So much for your Jew clothing. Show me your papers."

With a smirk, I pulled them out and handed them over. He scrutinized the documents then tossed them back at me. "Although your papers are in order and you speak German quite well, I'm not convinced. I believe people are guilty until proven innocent, and my gut and the circumstances indicate you are indeed an American." With a slight nod of his head, one of his goons thrust his rifle butt into my back. I grunted as the other goon pushed Veronika to start walking.

They directed us to a parked Kfz. 21 staff car, with its odd four rear wheels. We were shoved in the back while the *Scharführer* sat in the passenger's seat and his obedient boot-licker took the steering wheel. For good measure, another goon squeezed in beside me, pointing his Walther P38 in my face. With slits for headlights, we head out into the night.

By the time we reached our destination, dawn had illuminated the world into which we had now fallen. Wolfman's interrogation chamber was situated just on the outskirts of the Łódź Ghetto. Prodded to exit the vehicle at gunpoint, Veronika and I began walking along the cobbled street, side-stepping the trolley tracks, when Wolfie directed us to take a short detour. On the way he revealed his name, and Hans Schmidt gave us a brief history of his stellar rise in the glorious Third Reich. As a devout Hitler Youth and then soldier of the SA (Attack Division), Hans boasted about how in 1938 he had bashed in the windows of Jewish storefronts and the heads of whimpering Jews on *Kristallnacht*, with the pogrom's proud tally of 7000 businesses being utterly destroyed and 1000 synagogues burned to the ground throughout Germany and Austria. His ferocity was dully noted and promotions followed.

Parading us into the heart of the ghetto, Hans pointed to a dignified-looking older man with round spectacles wearing a handsome herringboned wool coat. He was beating an undernourished woman mercilessly with his riding crop while fellow citizens (also emaciated and destitute) just stood by, motionless and, quite astonishingly, lacking the will to intervene.

I gazed at Hans. "Who the hell is that creep?"

"He is King Chiam." Hans laughed mockingly. "Actually, he is Chiam Rumkowski, our prized Jewish kapo and president of the Jewish Council."

As Veronika watched this ruthless King of Jews beat his flock, her face reeked with venom. Following my lead, she asked in fluent German, "And what does a kapo do?"

Hans gazed at Veronika, his face stern, annoyed she had the temerity to even speak without his permission. He smacked his hand with his riding crop. "A kapo, *Fräulein*, is a filthy Jew who we make feel as if he is a German. Basically, kapos rule over their sty of worthless Jewish pigs under our watchful supervision."

Veronika's face contorted. "It must feel great to be a jackass emboldened to be a wolf, simply because you have a pack of deadly hyenas to protect you."

Hans lifted his riding crop and struck her across the face! I leapt and grabbed the whip with my free hand as a guard cracked me in the back of the head with the butt of his rifle. I fell to my knees while Veronika was inevitably dragged down beside me, our wrists red with pain. I glanced at her swollen face and sprang back on my feet, eyes blazing. I was itching to show Max Schmeling that I was Joe Louis, but had to wait for the right moment, as I spat, "So help me God, if you ever do that again, you will—"

"I *will* do whatever I please," Hans interrupted. "That's enough of your nonsense, and the end of this tour." Turning to one of his guards, he barked, "Take them to my chamber. *Mach Schnell!"*

As we had found out later, the Łódź Ghetto was one of many created in Poland by the Nazis due to poor planning. Immediately after the invasion of Poland in 1939, Heinrich Himmler and Adolf Eichmann had enacted an enormous relocation program, whereby dispossessing hundreds of thousands of Poles of their homes and businesses to hand over to the half million Germans that would Aryanize the newly-seized territory. At the same time Nazi soldiers were commandeering the businesses, homes, and valuable possessions of Polish Jews and had no place to put them. The mass confusion forced Himmler to change their initial plans and corral Jews into ghettos.

Reinhard Heydrich had opposed creating ghettos from the start, citing how ghettos, being isolated districts, were hard to police and bred criminals and rebels, not to mention disease. Nevertheless, thousands of Poles and Jews died in the process from starvation or disease. Yet that colossal mistake mattered little to the Nazis as Poles and Jews were subhuman anyhow, and massive death tolls now became a welcome side effect of their logistical failure.

One guard pushed us from behind while two others followed with Hans trailing behind. We entered a drab brick building, apparently an apartment complex that was transformed into a makeshift command center. As we were escorted down into the cellar, I realized that the lackluster exterior had actually been luxurious, for what we now entered was a dark and gloomy dungeon. The air was dank and the decaying brick walls were covered with mold. The clay and dirt floor was stained with blotches of various shades of scarlet and vermillion, apparently not from any form of paint.

In the far corner stood Hans's workbench. It contained an assortment of shears, saws, chisels, vices and chains. The tools were surprisingly all immaculate; my hope was that Hans was only a collector and not a fastidious cleaner of torture utensils. But that thought quickly evaporated when I spotted a jar of human body parts soaking in formaldehyde. Whether this was a scare tactic or not, I knew one thing for sure: Hans was an aberration, and had to be destroyed.

The guard adjusted our tied hands, now securing us in separate seats with our hands tied to the back of our chairs, which were then placed side by side. The two other SS guards stood behind us with their rifles cocked and ready. Hans finally made his grand entrance, gently slapping his riding crop against the palm of his hand. "Welcome to my confessional chamber."

I looked around. "I must confess…it's charming. Who's your decorator?"

Veronika tetchily elbowed me while Hans erupted! With volcanic rage, he whipped his workbench, causing the jar of body parts to tip over. It rolled and fell to the floor, shattering into a starburst of shards as an assortment of severed fingers, toes, and ears went careening across the floor.

"I'm sick of your flippant wisecracks! Now look what you made me do!" Hans screamed, his neck veins bulging and face fire-engine red.

Having elicited the desired reaction, I smiled. "You're a rookie, Hans. And when you find out who I am, you'll truly regret this imposition."

"Nice try," he said, straining to temper his response. "But you can't fool *me*. Yes, you're wearing civilian clothes and speak German, but you're not a German officer or even an Aryan. No German would be hunkered in the woods with a Night Witch. No, no, you're an American all right, and we have your B-24 plane wreckage to prove it." Hans turned his gaze toward Veronika. "And we have your Polikarpov piece of trash in cinders. So, where is your base?"

Veronika chuckled as she glanced at me. "You're right, he *is* a rookie!"

Hans slapped Veronika—*hard*.

My lips twisted in rage as Veronika retorted, "Slap me all you like. You're *not* going to get any military confessions out of *me*."

Hans exhaled and leaned against his workbench, gazing at the two of us, visibly humiliated and rethinking his tactics. He took several deep breaths and then asked calmly, "Very well, *Fräulein*, let's just start with a simple question, like where were you born?"

Veronika looked at me, and I nodded for her to answer, knowing he'd never be able to use any information we gave him. Hans didn't know it yet, but I had already engraved his headstone in my mind, replete with a border of poison ivy and two dead birds—a cuckoo and a loon.

Taking my cue, Veronika replied, "I was born in Azzano, Italy."

"Italy?" Hans retorted. "Are you a comedian, like your friend here?"

"No," Veronika replied. "My parents were both Italian. They moved to St. Petersburg, Russia when I was twelve years old. Our name changed from Scalia to Scaliakov."

Hans smiled. "You, *Fräulein*, are a liar! You think you can outsmart *me*? Ha! St. Petersburg no longer exists. So where do you *really* come from?"

Veronika smirked. "I wasn't trying to trick you. I simply refuse to acknowledge the city's new name. It was changed to Leningrad after the bloody revolution by the Bolsheviks."

As Hans's gloating face mellowed, Veronika gave us a succinct overview of the city's history, stating that prior to 1917 St. Petersburg had been the nation's capital. After Lenin's death, Stalin rose to power and turned a cultural epicenter, which was brimming with talent, into a stagnant city paralyzed with fear. Veronika's father had founded the successful Scaliakov Piano Shop, appropriately located on Italyanskaya St., and was friends with many great composers, including Sergei Prokofiev and Dmitri Shostakovich. However, in 1936, Russia was in the midst of the Great Terror as thousands were executed and millions sent to Gulags in Siberia. People were singled out for prison or execution by mere accusations by their neighbors or enemies, thus creating a terrifying atmosphere of uncertainty and looming death.

That same year, Stalin had criticized Shostakovich's avant-garde opera *Lady Macbeth*. To redeem himself, and save his skin, Dmitri composed his *Fifth Symphony*. His public declaration was that his symphony was "a Soviet artist's creative response to justified criticism."

In a final breath, Veronika declared, "Shostakovich had buckled to breathe, just like millions of others. While the rest are either imprisoned, intentionally starved or executed. And that's the hellish world Soviet-ruled Russia is today—a nation shackled in terror by Stalin. A place I no longer wish to call home."

I sat there, once again, not fully believing that Stalin is a monster. Perhaps there is a good deal of subversion going on; after all, any takeover of a nation involves reprisals by the losing faction, necessitating severe disciplinary actions. Yet, I had learned a few things I hadn't known.

Meanwhile, Hans Schmidt rubbed his chin and remarked, "Stalin is a fool. As Hitler said in his speech this past November 8, little Joseph stands in front of the curtain while his Jewish political minister, or rather *master*, Lazar Kaganovich pulls his strings—for it was Kaganovich who orchestrated your catastrophic famine in 1932 and enforced the grain confiscations that starved your people to death. But I commend Stalin or Lazar, whoever's idea it was, for cleansing your nation of dissidents, degenerates, and the disabled. No nation can be strong without taking such measures."

Veronika had been gritting her teeth as she listened, but now retorted, "Stalin is no puppet, and Kaganovich no angel. Both are monsters! So is that how Germany is handling *your* undesirables in the Łódź Ghetto? By starving them and having them beat and abuse one another?"

Hans laughed. "Exactly! You see Stalin and his Jewish advisors are all dimwitted, low-class laborers; they foolishly do all the dirty work themselves. Meanwhile, we superior Germans enlist a handful of degenerate Jews and give them just enough power to win their loyalty, while simultaneously prodding them and rewarding them to do our bidding. It is far more intelligent and gratifying to see a Jew abusing a Jew, or rather hundreds of thousands of Jews, while assisting us with our Final Solution."

Veronika and I responded simultaneously. "What's this Final Solution of yours?" I asked while she sarcastically jabbed, "Ah, so I see. Hitler pulls Hans's strings, so *Hans the puppet* can pull the Jewish kapo's strings." As Hans's face twisted, she added, "Your brainless pogrom of Jews, Hans, is not only idiotic it's also heinous! Especially since my mother happened to be an Italian Jew."

Hans's ears perked up! Veronika's *puppet* slur was indeed worthy of a flogging, but her shocking last sentence was a game changer. His face twisted with revulsion as he stood erect and exclaimed, "Ah ha! I couldn't have asked for a better confession. And you thought you were so clever, didn't you, you filthy mongrel." Venom surged through Hans's veins as he hissed, "Your interrogation, you insolent Jewish Night Witch, is over!" Turning to one of his guards, he barked, "Get her out of my sight! And see to it that she gets put on the next train to Auschwitz."

Veronika sat bewildered and mute as I yelled, "What the hell is going on here?"

An unnervingly sinister look distorted Hans's face as he turned his scorching eyes toward me, and cackled, "And *you* foolishly thought I was a rookie. Ha! I have you both where I want you. Your Jewish hybrid is going to a labor camp with the rest of her useless kind." He glanced at his tools and added, "While *you* will stay here with me for some fine tuning, or should I say, fine pruning!"

The guard was already dragging Veronika up the cellar steps, when I stared deep into Hans's eyes and barked, "You damn coward! Let me loose so we can deal with this man-to-man, rather than man-to-worm."

Hans laughed as the door slammed shut—Veronika was gone!

The demented *Scharführer* began slipping on a pair of leather gloves, very slowly, wriggling his fingers in a menacing claw-like manner. He turned his wild-eyed gaze back at me. "Well, I'm not foolish enough to let you loose, but I will honor your request for a one-on-one session." He turned toward his two remaining guards. "Leave us. *Schnell!*"

The two guards obediently followed orders and exited the dungeon, closing the thick wooden door behind them.

"There," Hans said as he picked up a pair of hedge shears. "Now it is just you and I."

5

Auschwitz

March 10, 1942

*I*t was the dawn of a new day and the beginning of Veronika's descent into Hitler's hell. The SS guard shoved Veronika through the dense crowd of Jewish men, women and children. All were tagged with a yellow Star of David with the word "Jude" emblazoned in the center. SS guards with machineguns lined the Łódź railway station while others roamed the crowd with German Shepherds. Despite some anxious murmurs and cries of children, the atmosphere was unnaturally calm and orderly as SS guards and kapos prodded hundreds of Polish Jews to climb aboard cattle cars.

Long lines formed, congesting the station. Men and women carrying any meager possessions or luggage they may have had bumped into each other as they boarded a seemingly endless row of linked trains. Guards carefully counted each prisoner as they boarded, packing them in tighter than the intended livestock. Once a railcar was full, the guard scribbled the head count on the wooden exterior with white chalk then slid the large doors closed.

Veronika grabbed the rusty metal handrail and pulled herself up into the human-cattle car, coming face-to-face with a bearded man with deep-set eyes, broken spectacles and bruises on his cheeks. Turning her gaze to the left, she connected with a pallid woman with sad eyes, unkempt blond hair, and a six-year-old boy clutching one arm and a four-year-old girl griping the other. Their cold, empty stares were unsettling—not only for the torment they had obviously witnessed and experienced but because they mirrored those of every other person stuffed into these godforsaken cattle cars. Despite the vast majority being Jews, there were several Protestants, Catholics and Jehovah's Witnesses.

As the large wooden door slid closed behind her, Veronika jerked. Meanwhile, the damning sound of the lock nailed home the finality of their one-way journey to a wretched world, one filled with uncertainty and despair. The train bucked and began rolling toward its destination some 170 miles south, near the southern border of occupied Poland. The cattle cars reeked of the smelly animals that had previously been carted and of the many disheveled passengers forced to live in squalor, and without windows, the putrid smell festered.

Veronika covered her nose, but soon realized it was futile. She would have to begin acclimating herself to the awful smell, for it was but only a prelude to the rancid new life that awaited. Her mind was consumed with foreboding when the bearded man broke her spell. "Why are you here? You wear expensive clothes and have no star."

The train rocked and swayed as Veronika steadied herself and replied, "Yes, no Star of David and no Northern Star to guide me out of this purgatory and into the hands of Christ."

The man squinted. "So are you a Christian or Jew?"

"My father was Roman Catholic and my mother was Jewish, but she converted and I was raised Catholic."

The bearded man's left eyebrow rose. "My cousin lives in Slovakia, the president of which is Josef Tiso, who just so happens to be a Catholic priest."

Veronika didn't see the connection, but figured the man was just trying to make conversation as she politely replied, "Oh, I didn't know that. How nice."

"No! It is *not* nice," the man carped, his demeanor now indignant. "Hitler and his bloodthirsty hounds have recently demanded that Slovakia deport all their Jews. And your Catholic priest has literally *sold* us out!"

"Hold on!" Veronika retorted. "*My* priest? You're being presumptuous. Don't brand every Catholic priest as being like this Tiso fellow."

As the train continued to chug and belch through the brisk March air, heads turned to their rousing debate. The man nodded. "Yes, perhaps you're right. Do excuse me, but you see I received a disturbing letter yesterday from my cousin Calev's wife. She said a massive pogrom is currently under way. The Slovakian government has willingly adopted Hitler's vile policy of commandeering the businesses and homes of Jews. They had burst into their home and dragged Calev out, ordering his family to pack and be ready to move out by the following day, and to leave behind all their valuable possessions. Meanwhile, Calev was shoved onto a Nazi train. Its destination: Auschwitz!"

As Veronika and others gasped, he continued, "Evidently, Tiso, the Catholic priest, negotiated a lucrative deal with the Devil. He has allowed Hitler to take all of Slovakia's Jews, except their possessions. Moreover, Tiso will pay Hitler 500 Reichsmarks for each Jew taken. And where will this money come from? Simple! Tiso's Hlinka guards are vigorously hunting down and robbing these Jews to pay his evil partner and to fill his own coffer. If other nations follow this precedent, the entire Jewish population will be thrust into utter destitution and eventually be eradicated from existence. The world has truly gone mad!"

Passengers shuddered at the horrifying news as the woman with two children interjected, "Please! You are scaring my children." Gazing down at her son, she instructed, "Duriel, *don't* listen!" Then to her daughter, "You too, Neta."

The bearded man glanced at the woman and down at her anxious children as Veronika responded, "While I agree we are living in perhaps the most evil time in history, you all must know that the righteous far exceed the wicked, as one bad apple cannot truly spoil the orchard. And the Allies have united to end this ungodly madness. They did so for World War I, and they will do so again." Then came her impassioned finale, "So, my friends, do *not* lose hope!"

Veronika knew in her heart that she herself was losing faith. The Nazis seemed invincible. But the little poem her father had written exclusively for her as a child always managed to lift her spirits and bring a smile to her face.

When times are the most bleak,
It is crucial to speak,
Not about what is wrong,
But how one remains strong.
Hence, the best way to cope,
Is to never lose hope.

The smile Veronika now wore, however, was for more than her father's poem; it was for the many passengers who applauded her words of encouragement. Acknowledging her appreciation, she then asked that they all join in a silent prayer as each bowed their head and communed with their God. Afterward, the Jews began singing the "Hatikvah."

The trek seemed never ending as the monotonous clickety–clack of steel wheels on rails seemed to echo the grave sound of the clock, ticking their freedom away with each ominous clank. Then they felt the train come to an alarming stop. Gazing at each other, racked with fear, many hoped that the malodorous train ride would have lasted until the madness of war ended. Life, from here forward, they knew, would never be the same again.

Then the doors abruptly slid open! SS guards wielding batons bellowed orders to disembark while cattle-prodding them to separate into groups of men and women. Several guards began beating prisoners across their backs, others on their heads, and those whom they simply didn't like their looks, across their faces, while barking, "Hurry, you dogs! Get in line!" *SS Helferinnen* (women guards) walked through the masses, eyeing up the women while SS guards inspected the men. Visible strength was the determining factor; those capable of hard labor would remain, while those deemed too weak (which included infants and children up to eight years old and most people over forty) would now follow the new protocol established by Reinhard Heydrich and Heinrich Himmler at the Wannsee Conference. Namely, they would be exterminated immediately.

Those culled for extermination stood petrified and baffled as SS guards eyed them up like meat in a market. Some guards brutishly grabbed and shoved them toward the killing ground while others initiated the new protocol of their commandant, namely, they deceptively lulled them with lies.

One guard reveled in the deceitful role-playing as he declared, "Welcome to Auschwitz, ladies. Our camp is dedicated to cleanliness, and you and your children will receive nice warm showers in our new facility. So, please, remove all your clothing." As the women's faces blanched with a mixture of humiliation and embarrassment, the guard continued, "Now, now, ladies. Don't be shy. God gave you all the same body parts. Fold your clothes neatly and tie your shoes together with their laces. We want to make sure everything gets returned to you in good order."

As the remaining *acceptable* prisoners were escorted toward the main camp, they nervously looked up. Looming before them was the wrought iron entrance gate to Auschwitz. Emblazoned across the top was a slogan; it read *"Arbeit Macht Frei"* (Work Makes Freedom). As they crossed the threshold, however, their nervous hearts simmered to the soothing sounds of Schubert's rollicking scherzo from his *Ninth Symphony*. There, in a courtyard near the kitchen, a small orchestra was playing with warm abandon. Many prisoners bowed their heads, praying that Auschwitz was indeed merely a labor camp. However, the gruesome reality was to be much darker, for it would take more than just work to gain one's freedom: it would take an indomitable will of steel—or a miracle.

As they filtered into the camp, Veronika gazed down the main pathway. It was lined with several rows of two-storied, redbrick buildings, fairly mundane in appearance, yet looking harmlessly enough like ordinary apartments. She sighed with relief as her eyes then spotted an inmate sweeping one of the side pathways. He was middle aged, extremely thin, wearing a striped uniform, and had on a pair of mismatched shoes without laces that were caked with dried mud. Veronika squinted with curiosity. Peering around her, she then slipped away from the confusion and approached the man from behind. "Excuse me, sir," she whispered, "but what *truly* goes on in this place?"

The man hesitated, but then turned his head slightly in her direction. "My advice, dear woman, is this: Just be kind to them. That just *might* save you."

"Save me from what?"

Just then Veronika felt a crack on the back of her head. With a grunt she spun around to see a scrawny little SS officer with thick glasses, beady eyes, and blond hair. He stood in a lordly manner, with one hand planted firmly on his tiny hip and the other wielding his well-used riding crop.

"Get in line!" the *Sturmbannführer* snapped.

"Which line?"

He eyed her up, a smile of surprise etching his gaunt weasel-like face. "Well, what do we have here? You are not only physically fit, *Fräulein*, but have two other redeeming qualities. You are very beautiful and wear no star." He rubbed his chin. "Yes, *you* I shall assign to my personal quarters to perform light duty."

Veronika glanced at the inmate, whose expression indicated that she take the offer. Gazing back into the weasel's lustful eyes, she queried, "And what exactly is light duty?"

His eyes twinkled as his bony hand returned to his lanky little hip. "My dear, any wench would flock to do Klaus Becker's paperwork or work in the kitchen." His eyes undressed her. "And I'm sure you'd prepare a great meal for me. After all, you're a pretty nice dish yourself."

"And you're a pig," Veronika retorted.

The inmate vigorously shook his head. "No, no! Please, *Sturmbannführer* Becker, don't harm her. She's new."

Klaus swung his crop around, smashing the man in the face. The man screamed in pain, dropped the broom, and held his swollen cheek as blood oozed from his split lip.

Klaus barked, "*Ruhe* (silence), you dog!"

Veronika attempted to console the beaten man when Becker grabbed her wrist. "You are very lucky you are beautiful, *Fräulein,* and not a Jew! Otherwise I would have sent you straight to the Little Red House."

"And what *is* this Little Red Riding House of yours?" Veronika sardonically snapped.

Klaus didn't appreciate her cocky, childish insult, especially considering the severe nature of the building, but he was enamored by her beauty as he retorted, "It happens to be a special little cottage that we customized specifically for undesirables. Know this, *Fräulein*: I do *not* tolerate insolence, so mind your tongue. Or else—"

Just then a *Blockführerin* approached Klaus, telling him to report immediately to Rudolf Höss, the camp commandant. Angrily, he glanced at the female block leader and back at Veronika as he released her hand. "I will deal with you later. Now get back in line with the other women. *Schnell!*"

As Klaus took his leave with the *Blockführerin*, Veronika defiantly stood her ground and turned back toward the battered inmate. "What is this Little Red House?"

The man nervously looked both ways to ensure their privacy, and whispered, "It is a little brick cottage that was recently renovated. The windows and doors were bricked up, while its interior was divided into two large airtight chambers, each with an entrance door."

Veronika squinted. "Airtight chambers? What in God's name are those for?"

"Well," The man hesitated. "You see, they also built two small hatches, placed high on the brick wall, one for each chamber. And, and, I don't know if I s-should tell you," he stammered.

She grasped his arm. "Please, you must. What goes on there?"

The man swallowed hard. "You seem like a very nice lady and I truly don't wish to frighten the daylights out of you. Why don't you just do what they tell you and hope this war ends soon, like the rest of us?"

"That's not my nature. That's why. I'm a *vigoroso Italiano,* as my father used to say. So, please, tell me what those hatches are for?"

The man hesitated once again, but relented. "They use those hatches to drop in crystals...crystals of Zyklon-B."

Again, Veronika squinted. "What is that? A disinfectant to cleanse the prisoners?"

The man's face withered into an abysmal sullen state as he murmured, "No, my dear, Zyklon-B is crystallized prussic acid." His voice rose into a crescendo of angst. "It is a form of cyanide used to exterminate insects, but these evil butchers have now decided to exterminate *us!*"

Veronika gasped, her face flush with shock. "Dear God! That can't be! You must be mistaken."

"No, my dear, I am not." Tears filled his eyes as he struggled to continue. "My friends and I were forced to build those two god-awful death chambers, not realizing their intended use. Yet upon completion, my friends were the first specimens these bastards used to test out their hideous gas chambers."

"That's awful! No, it's *insane!*" Veronika's eyes rolled randomly, trying to comprehend the unfathomable dimensions of the Nazis' barbarous insanity. *Hitler is certainly guilty,* she thought, *being the mastermind. But what about his evil henchmen and henchwomen? They're the ones in the killing trenches willingly carrying out his diabolical orders.* Her eye twitched. *To speak of evil is one thing, to execute evil is another. Where is their willpower? Or their consciences?* Her mind then returned to the inmate's harrowing personal story as she gazed back into his tortured eyes. "But how on Earth did *you* manage to survive?"

"I'm not proud of this but, as I advised you, I do *whatever* they ask." His head dropped.

Just then the bone-jarring cries of children and terrified wails of their mothers shrieked behind them. Turning toward the upheaval, Veronika saw SS guards and *SS Helferinnen* pulling children away from their mothers. Amid the hysteria one child ran away from a guard and clutched onto Veronika's skirt. Shocked, Veronika glanced down at the young boy. It was Duriel, the boy she had seen on the train. The guard ran over and attempted to tear the boy away, yet Veronika's skirt lifted, still being in the clutches of Duriel's little fingers. Veronika grasped Duriel's hand and then stared menacingly into the guard's eyes. "What are you doing!?"

The guard continued to pull on the boy with both hands as he barked, "I'm taking him and his kin to the Little Red House. They need to be deloused. Now, *let go!*" The guard reached down into his holster with one hand and pulled out his Luger.

Veronika glanced over to see Duriel's mother and sister being dragged away. Her heart dropped and her mind raced. She knew they were chosen—no longer by Yahweh, but rather by Hitler—to be exterminated, and she had to intervene. She now knew that in this nightmarish world where light is dark and dark is darker she had to think differently. On pure instinct, she ripped Duriel away from the guard and snapped, "Leave him alone! This boy is *my* son. I've been searching everywhere for him."

Perplexed, the guard paused, then lowered his pistol. "What do you mean? He was standing over there with his mothe—uh, that woman and her daughter."

Veronika glanced down at Duriel; who gazed up at her with fear in his eyes, trembling. Speaking in Polish, she said, "Don't worry, darling. This man will not harm you. I'll protect you." Peering back up at the guard, she said in German, "As you can see, I am not a Jew. Some Jewish bitch must have tried to kidnap my son and put this hideous star on him." She ripped the star off.

The guard appreciated her anti-Semitic venom, but remained skeptical. "Whom might you be, *Frau*?"

"My name is Veronika Scalia. I'm Italian by birth but had moved to Poland six years ago. How I ended up here," she spat, "is a question I'm still asking!"

The guard's demeanor mellowed. "I cannot answer that, but I think it's best if I escort you to the commandant. He'll know best what to do with you and your son."

The guard turned, aiming to ensure that the massive crowd was still under control. Meanwhile, Veronika glanced and winked at the battered inmate, who shook his head with a smile, appreciating her brazen method of dealing with barbarians.

The guard turned back. "Come with me."

As they walked through the frenzied crowd teaming with men, women and children being ruthlessly torn from their families, Veronika was sweating—not only from the intense encounter, but also from the unpleasant climate. Auschwitz had been built near a wetland sitting on the confluence of the Sola and Vistula Rivers. The climate was routinely muggy and often unbearable, which only added to the misery.

The guard plowed through a dense crowd of anxious prisoners being directed to disrobe. Women and men were lined up for the next phase, namely the demoralizing process of dehumanizing them. Issued colorless, gray and charcoal-striped clothes, they then had their hair completely shaven off. The loss of their names was the final insult as guards tattooed numbers on their arms and entered their numeric identities into the register. Veronika gazed in disbelief as they walked past a long row of low redbrick buildings, eventually arriving at the commandant's office. The guard cordially opened the door to allow Veronika and the boy to enter, but as they did, Veronika's eyes lit up. Standing before her was Klaus Becker. The malicious little *Sturmbannführer* was speaking to the commandant, when suddenly he turned, a smile sweeping across his licentious face. "Ah, my insolent beauty. So we meet again," he said in his shrilly voice.

Veronika froze as the *SS Rottenführer* guard at her side saluted his superiors and asked, "*Sturmbannführer* Becker, you know this woman?"

"*Ya, ya,*" Klaus replied. "Send her in."

Veronika stepped in slowly, with Duriel latched to her side, as Klaus glanced at Rudolf Höss. "This is the spirited apparition of Freyja I spoke of, Commandant."

Höss, who was a small man in stature and content to have never acquired a conscience, gazed at Veronika and then down at the boy, his face steely hard and his eyes dead cold, like a shark's. He glanced at Becker. "Never mind the silly Nordic goddess of beauty nonsense. What is her situation?"

Klaus smirked as he glanced at the guard standing by the door. "What have you learned?"

"She is Italian, sir. Veronika Scalia. Moved to Poland six years ago and somehow ended up here with her son."

"Very well, *Rottenführer,* at ease," Klaus commanded.

"No!" Höss interjected, "Report back to your station, *Rottenführer,* and continue processing today's arrivals. *Obersturmbannführer* Eichmann has just telephoned, and our new schedule has been significantly augmented. Moving forward, one thousand prisoners will be arriving by rail *daily.*"

His face intensified. "And with Auschwitz II/Birkenau now operational, I expect this camp to begin processing prisoners much more efficiently!"

Auschwitz II/Birkenau was located three kilometers away in a particularly dreary and smelly marshland that no one, except Himmler and Höss, would ever deem suitable. Yet to fulfill Hitler's ambitious decree to begin exterminating Jews en masse the project had hastily commenced. Birkenau, however, was to be nothing like the main camp, or any other prison camp previously built, whose purpose was to merely contain prisoners. Birkenau was designed specifically to be one thing only: a death factory to *kill* prisoners.

Operation Reinhard was the Nazis' plan to exterminate the two plus million Jews in the General Government (The German occupied areas of Poland and Russia), and thus called for inventive new methods to facilitate rapid and efficient liquidations. With the rival camps at Bełżec and Sobibór being built, Höss had made visits to glean ideas, thus helping him solve problems he experienced at the main camp. A major issue at Auschwitz was that the crematorium was located too close to the barracks, requiring them to rev motorcycle engines to conceal the screams of prisoners who spotted the incinerators. As such, Höss strategically located the crematorium at Birkenau out of sight, whereby not alerting new arrivals to the imminent mass murder that awaited them. That change along with coaxing prisoners with calm deception rather than brute force helped to subdue the panic experienced at the main camp, which in turn had caused hysterical outbreaks and impeded production. And production was paramount to Höss, a man who took great pride in comparing his camp's efficiency levels to those of his rivals.

Veronika's face paled. It didn't take much for her to figure out that this new Birkenau facility was a human slaughterhouse. She pulled Duriel close to her, but suddenly flinched as the guard behind her clicked his heels and barked, "Heil Hitler!"

The *Rottenführer* obediently departed, keeping the wheels of madness turning, as Klaus unexpectedly bent down and stroked the boy's hair. "So, what is your name, son?"

Duriel stood petrified and mute as Veronika answered, "Donato."

Klaus stood up. "Does he not speak when spoken to?"

"Not when he can't understand your language."

"Ah!" Klaus said, "I know a little Italian." Looking at the boy, he asked, *"Come ti chiami?"*

Again, Duriel (aka Donato) stood mute. Klaus's eye twitched as he stared at Veronika, his mind filling with suspicion. "What is this? Some sort of prank or is it an outright lie? Whose son *is* this?"

"As you've been told, *Sturmbannführer*, he is mine. You were also told that I moved to Poland six years ago. My son, as you can see, is no more than six years old, is he? Hence, he never learned to speak Italian."

Höss interjected, *"Sturmbannführer* Becker, enough! Leave her be. She is obviously the boy's mother. Let's focus on what we intend to do with them."

Klaus glanced at Höss and then back at Veronika. Not only did he not like her condescending tone or brazen spirit, he also didn't like her fishy story either. As he gazed at her pretty, clever face, his mind churned her fish tale into chum. *You may have managed to win Höss's approval,* his mind reeled, *but you will not win the next argument; namely, where you will be sent!* Klaus looked back at Höss and declared firmly, "I am separating these two charlatans; she assigned to hard labor, and the boy—"

"That's outrageous," Veronika interjected. "I'm Italian, and a military ally. You *must* release us both immediately!"

Klaus abruptly raised his hand to thrash her, but Donato kicked him in the shin. With a yelp, Klaus boiled with rage as he bent over, rubbed his shin, and spat, "I'm sick of this bitch and this mysterious boy!" He grabbed his riding crop off of Höss's desk and was about to flog them, when Höss stood up and shouted, "I said *enough!* This woman and her son have both made a fool of you. And you have turned my office into a circus." Planting his two fists, knuckles down, firmly on his desk, Höss leaned forward and added, "Moreover, *I* make the final decisions around here, *not you!* Is that understood, *Sturmbannführer* Becker?"

"*Ja voll, meine* Commandant!" Klaus barked in frustration.

Höss leaned back and crossed his arms. Exhaling a deep breath, he then stared at Klaus with supreme gravity. "Veronika and Donato shall be treated as detainees until I get to the bottom of this. I will make inquiries to the Italian embassy. In the interim, she will be an aide to my staff. She and her son will occupy a single bed in the prison barracks nearest to my office. Is that understood?"

Klaus's lips twisted as he grudgingly replied, "Yes. It shall be done, *meine* Commandant."

Veronika flashed a mocking smile at Klaus and then demurely looked at Höss. "*Danke*, Commandant Höss."

Klaus's blood curdled.

Veronika enjoyed a modicum of tranquility over the next two weeks, performing clerical work with mostly women in Höss's office. Her unmolested state being primarily due to the new conditions outside her office's protective walls. In short, Klaus Becker was inundated with the rapid new flow of arrivals, not to mention all the departures to another realm.

However, evading Becker's volatile temper didn't offer Veronika peace of mind. For within the walls of her office and barracks at night she heard horrific tales of the debauchery occurring within the main camp, as well as the new Birkenau facility, each shutting out the sane world with their 13-foot-high electrified fences.

While filing papers or licking and pasting stamps on envelopes Veronika overheard several meetings in Rudolf Höss's office, some startling and others terrifying.

Evidently, Heinrich Himmler's original plan to deal with the Jews had simply been one of relocation. All Jews would be sent to Africa; territory the Germans believed would be conquered in record time by their superior *Luftwaffe* and Panzer divisions. However, on December 11, 1941, Hitler declared war on the United States (venting his vitriolic belief that international Jewry had incited a world conflict by manipulating FDR, as they had Stalin). The Führer's brazen decision, however, elicited an unforeseen backlash, as American forces joined the British to oust Rommel's Panzers from the African continent. With Himmler's proposed Judaic dumping ground humiliatingly destroyed, the *Reichsführer* had no option but to change his previously assured plan, particularly since Hitler's rhetoric intensified as the *Führer* had finally made public his hidden obsession, namely the *extermination of all Jews*. That chilling directive, coupled with Himmler's failed Polish, German and Jewish relocation plan, suddenly made Auschwitz and other camps appear like the ideal solution. That Himmler didn't have the materials, money or manpower to perform the gargantuan feat didn't matter. He would order his underlings to improvise, namely steal from the vanquished Poles or even from their fellow competing prisoner camps.

Simultaneously, Hitler and Goering had planned on a rapid victory with their invincible *blitzkrieg* to conquer Russia before the winter of 1941. Yet despite an impressive start, Operation Barbarossa had likewise turned into a dismal failure as their assault dragged into the winter and thousands of ill-equipped Nazis froze to death during the inglorious Battle of Moscow. The synthetic rubber factory that Nazi leaders intended to build in Russia now had to be built elsewhere. Given that they captured a staggering two-and-a-half-million Soviet prisoners, Auschwitz, once again, seemed like the ideal solution. In response, Soviet POWs were thrust into slavery. Forced at gunpoint, they would build the Nazis' new synthetic rubber factory and expand the Auschwitz complex.

The plight of Soviet POWs, Veronika learned, would be far greater than mere slavery. They were the first prisoners in Germany to be tattooed a number (originally across their chest, but then placed on their arms due to the intense pain of the former method), and were the first to be literally worked to death through strenuous hard labor and starvation. Hundreds of thousands of others were slaughtered outright. Due to Stalin's failure to recognize international law, Soviet soldiers were exempt from the protection of the Geneva Convention. As such, Hitler issued the Commissar Order. This conveniently authorized Nazi soldiers to kill Soviet POWs in cold blood.

Due to the large number of captives that the Germans could not feed, nor had facilities to incarcerate, Soviet POWs were forced at gunpoint by the *Einsatzgruppen* or "Special Action Squads" to dig large pits. They were then lined up along the precipice as the *Einsatzgruppen* loaded their pistols and summarily shot them, one after another, in the back of the head at close range. As the prisoners' heads exploded, their limp bodies fell efficiently into their own mass grave.

Veronika had shuddered at hearing these chilling tales, especially since there seemed to be no end to how barbaric the Nazis could be. Another grim tale followed, illuminating how the Nazis rewarded the hundreds of thousands of Soviet POWs who had built the factory and other structures in the camp. They would be murdered via experimental methods of asphyxiation. The first method occurred in Chelmno, Poland, and entailed corralling the undressed victims into the back of a large truck, its rear compartment having been modified to be airtight. Hidden under the wood-grating floorboards were the truck's rerouted exhaust pipes. As the truck was driven two miles away to the mass gravesite in the forest, the Soviet soldiers choked and defecated in panic, dying of carbon monoxide poisoning.

However, the Nazis soon realized the truck's tiny rear compartment was insufficient; hundreds of thousands, not sixty, needed to be exterminated. Meanwhile, the exhaust fumes posed a twofold flaw: it took too long to asphyxiate humans and there was a psychological backlash on some Nazi soldiers, who had suffered depression, alcoholism or even committed suicide after listening to the Soviets suffer. The screams, choking, defecating, and scratching at the door for twenty minutes until they fell dead, was unbearable.

Through trial and error, however, the Nazis had learned how to build an efficient gas chamber and realized that Zyklon-B was the gas of choice. Hence, the Germans had finally arrived at the ultimate solution, one that could now be used on other undesirables for their Final Solution.

For many sleepless nights Veronika wriggled in bed as chilling visions of the horrors committed in the camp and on her former Soviet comrades unnerved her. Despite her loathing of Stalin and his corrupt regime, she had befriended many of the dictator's unfortunate and innocent pawns of war. Bad enough, she thought, they had lived in total fear under Stalin, but now they had fallen into the murderous hands of Hitler's ruthless henchmen to suffer unimaginably gruesome deaths. Added to this was the horrific realization that the gassings have continued, except it would now be primarily Jews and undesirables being exterminated, and on an accelerated scale that was utterly frightening.

Veronika tried to purge the horrendous visions from her mind, but there was another disturbing issue that plagued her daily. Poor little Donato was suffering his own hell. Having been separated from his mother and sister (not to mention his father, who mysteriously disappeared eight months earlier), Donato's whimpers in the night were coupled with his constant yearning to see his mother and sister, which, for survival reasons, Veronika had to prevent him from speaking about in public.

However, by April 23, Donato had begun to accept Veronika's assurance that he would one day be reunited with his family. Even Veronika took solace in the fact that she was not telling him a full-fledged lie, for being devoutly religious she knew that little Donato would indeed see them again, yet not on this godforsaken planet. To ensure Donato had a chance to survive, in the event that she were killed, Veronika gave Donato her elegant brooch, which he marveled over and carefully hid.

The next day Veronika tried her best to divert her thoughts while working in the office. Yet as she collated envelopes, her mind drifted into another black pit of pain as she wondered what gruesome fate befell Jack Goodwin at the hands of Hans Schmidt. Their time together had been brief, but somehow she could feel now that his presence had been a breath of fresh air, a warm refreshing presence of love perhaps—a love that now burned inside her, yearning to be back in his arms. And, *Dear God!* her mind cried, the pain of missing his presence.

Inadvertently, her tear-filled eyes veered toward the window, shattering her love dream—it was Klaus Becker! The intimidating *Sturmbannführer* was walking through the courtyard toward the administrative office. Veronika blinked hard, relinquishing her fanciful love-tear to the stoic swipe of her hand as hell rushed back into view. Nervously, she shifted in her chair, constrained by hesitation. Veronika had previously managed to avoid Klaus by slipping out of the office or her barracks, but today Rudolf Höss demanded that she complete her task before noon. Anxiously, she gazed at the clock. It was 11:30 and she still had a solid half hour of work left. She peered back at Höss, who was on the telephone and in eyeshot of her. Intuitively, she rose up, but then oscillated with indecision.

Just then, Klaus strolled in. Noticing her trepidation, his cadaverous face broadened with a malicious smile. "Ah, planning on going somewhere?"

"Uh…no. Just…stretching my legs."

"And what beautiful legs they are."

Veronika lips twisted. "You're redundant, *Sturmbannführer* Becker."

Klaus walked toward her and placed his hand on her back. "And you're ravishing yet repulsive, Veronika. Sit!"

Pushing her down, his skeletal hand rubbed her back—lustfully, harshly, then snuck around to massage her breast. Veronika clutched his hand and bit his finger! Klaus yelped and grabbed her neck with both hands, his long bony fingers like talons of a vulture strangling its prey. As she choked and struggled Höss slammed the telephone down and strode over. "What's going on?" he blasted.

Klaus released her. "This bitch is a damned she-wolf!"

Before Veronika could utter a word, Klaus continued, "*Meine* Commandant, I know you are besieged with many demands, so I had taken the liberty of doing some research for you."

Höss crossed his arms. "How considerate of you, *Sturmbannführer* Becker. And what research might that be? Could it be about locating the materials we desperately need to renovate and operate this camp? Or, perhaps, how we can process prisoners more efficiently?"

"No, Commandant. It pertains to your little vermin here, Veronika Scalia. I have been making numerous inquiries to the Italian consulate and have finally unearthed the truth."

Veronika's eyes widened as Höss uncrossed his arms, his curiosity now piqued. "Go on," he instructed.

A vindictive smile contorted Klaus's face as his beady eyes, embedded behind thick spectacles, glanced at Veronika then back toward Höss. "The records indicate that she was indeed born in Italy. However, her mother was a *Jew*." Höss recoiled and Veronika twitched as Klaus smugly continued, "And there is more. Her family then moved. *Not* to Poland, as she claimed, but to the Soviet Union. So you have before you, *meine* Commandant, a *Russian Jew!* Guilty on *both* accounts."

Höss's eyebrows rose as he turned his now menacing face toward Veronika. "Is this so? And I warn you, Veronika, you had better not lie, or you will suffer more than you can ever imagine."

Veronika could feel the adrenalin running through her veins as she glanced at Klaus, humiliated. Her fiendish foe had finally won. She closed her eyes briefly, willing her nerves to simmer down. She would have to face this calamity one way or another, and she decided to speak her piece. Opening her eyes, she said, "Working here I *can* imagine the worst suffering imaginable, because *you* soulless monsters are executing the most heinous atrocity known to mankind!"

Klaus snickered at her accusation and turned toward Höss, his face beaming with gratification. "I told you this Jew bitch was a liar!"

St. Louis, Missouri
September 20, 1957

"Oh my God!" Eleanor exclaimed as she anxiously leaned forward on the couch. "I can't believe she got caught."

"Yes, Klaus was a nasty piece of work all right," I said.

"It seems like the entire world was wicked back then. And you didn't even get to Alois Richter yet."

"Yes, don't worry," I said, as I lit another Camel. "Alois will enter this sordid tale soon enough. But—"

"And," Eleanor excitedly trampled over my words, "you never finished telling me what happened to you when that creep Hans Schmidt pulled out those hedge shears?"

I smiled as I blew a stream of nicotine out of my nostrils into the air. "Well, I'll get back to that. But as I told you, this is a long story, Ellie." I glanced at the exquisite grandfather clock that I had pinched from a wealthy Gestapo officer's abandoned estate during the chaotic aftermath of the war when the guilty rats fled; it was 7:22 P.M. "Perhaps I should finish this tale some other time, it's getting late."

Eleanor clutched my arm. "No way! You're not going anywhere, Daddio. You can't leave me hanging with Mom in this predicament."

I smiled. "Very well," I said as my face intuitively deadened. "But you had better sit back." My voice turned solemn. "Because it gets uglier. Much uglier and very, very dark. Auschwitz was Hell on Earth."

6

Hell on Earth

April 24, 1942

*C*ommandant Rudolf Höss couldn't believe his ears: First, to be told that Veronika lied, and was not only a Soviet enemy but also part Jewish. And second, to be insulted by her in such a humiliating manner was simply too much. His eyes glowed red, like Mars, the Bringer of War. "You are a liar and an insolent wench!" he spat. "Klaus was right all along." Turning toward Klaus, he said, "Your diligence, *Sturmbannführer* Becker, is highly commendable. As such, I award you full honors in deciding her fate, even if you deem putting a bullet in her head appropriate."

Klaus smiled, his thin lips creasing his gaunt cheeks as he took a deep breath to collect his thoughts. He paused but a moment, then declared, "*Danke, meine* Commandant. Although a bullet would be very gratifying, the elation would dissipate much too quickly." He turned his sinister gaze at Veronika. "No, no, my dear Soviet Jew bitch, you will not leave this planet that easily. Given that you just had to stick your big Jew nose into our business, I think it would be most appropriate that you *join* our business. Mind you, we've only given this grueling and gruesome task to males, namely criminals in the Reich or Ukrainians, as the Slavs are brutish animals anyhow. But you, my dear, have earned it. Your task will be to lug the cadavers from the gas chambers to the incinerator."

Veronika couldn't hold back any longer. "You are *sick!* All of you! You can have your sadistic way with me, but let Donato go."

"You are in *no* position to ask anything!" Klaus barked, his beady eyes vibrating in anger. Veronika's audacity and now tainted bloodline were too much, detonating the bomb within, as he spat, "You people just don't get it. We Germans are sick indeed—*sick of you!* You are *nothing.* Your people are *nothing.* And soon there will be *nothing left* of your entire subhuman race. Do I make myself clear?"

"Oh, yes, crystal clear. You're clearly out of your mind!"

Klaus short-circuited and slapped her hard across the face.

Veronika stood defiantly still, suppressing the pain, thus further humiliating Klaus. He clenched his teeth and hands while his body quaked with animus. In a fit of volcanic rage he slapped her again—*harder.* Veronika's head snapped sideways but sprang back. Defiantly, she remained silent and wiped the blood away from her lip. Klaus's fingers sprang out like switchblades as he stood in a lurch, contemplating mutilating her with his own bare hands.

Höss intervened. *"Sturmbannführer* Becker, enough! Your pathetic loss of control is unbefitting a German officer. This woman, this inferior half-Jew, has derailed you and is getting the better of you."

Klaus's heart was racing like a BMW 328 as he shook his head free of Veronika's hex, infuriated to have lost control in front of his superior. "I apologize, *meine*

Commandant, but this woman is like no other. She's incorrigible!"

"Indeed, she is," Höss replied. "It is clear, *Sturmbannführer* Becker, that I must rescind my last offer. I will not tolerate a prisoner unhinging a German officer in this camp. If seen in public it would set a bad example for our fellow officers and, worse yet, set a bad precedent for our prisoners. And—"

"But, Commandant," Klaus interjected, "I won't—"

"Yes, you *won't* be handling this matter any longer," Höss countered emphatically. "As it is, this raises another issue that concerns me. I abhor the way you and your men handle new arrivals, especially those who are culled for immediate extermination. The belligerent abuse and beatings must be replaced with calm, soothing deception. We've had sixty-seven hysterical outbursts yesterday that incited chaos due to separating mothers from their children and wives from husbands. We must keep families together. They must feel secure that they are in a labor camp, not a crematorium."

Veronika closed her eyes and bit her bloody lip. She had all to do to hold back from lashing out at these sadistic savages, who spoke of exterminating humans as if mere insects. But having won a minor success of unhinging Klaus and ending his reign over her, she didn't wish to push her luck with Höss and get an instant death sentence.

Meanwhile, Höss turned his heated gaze toward *her.* "As for you, *Frau* Scalia, it defies the Nazi Party's moral code to give a woman a man's job, as that, too, would set a bad precedent and upset the natural order of things. I abhor women who even contemplate doing a man's job. It is not only undignified, but it clearly exhibits an aberration of their genes."

Höss loathed women like Guida Diehl who had made spectacles of themselves by preaching to German women the dangers of feminism, while also organizing movements. Although agreeing with Diehl about the dangers of the unholy trinity (namely America's degenerate liberal Jewish culture, materialism, and the international Jewish conspiracy to control the world via the use of capitalism or subversion), Diehl, Höss believed, was simply a man in woman's clothing, or a lesbian. Either way, she was a genetic defect that warranted either sterilization or even extermination. However, a Jewish kapo punishing Jewish women, no matter how severe, was of little concern, as they were all subhuman animals anyhow.

"As the Nazi Party had professed," Höss continued, "a woman's place is in the nursery with children and in the kitchen. As such, *you*, Veronika, will work in the kitchen. And—"

"The *kitchen*?" Klaus interrupted. "Commandant, this woman is not only an enemy of the Reich, but also a half-Jew and a full-fledged liar. She cannot be trusted."

"I'm well aware of that, *Sturmbannführer* Becker," Höss said as he grasped his cap off the coatrack. "But I have no intentions of being duped again or letting her do light duty in the kitchen. She will be placed under the rigorous command of Kapo Bronislaw Sinkowski. He knows very well how to handle unruly Jewish women. This is not something we Germans should degrade ourselves with. Moreover, this will serve as a lesson to *you*, *Sturmbannführer* Becker, to not be outdone by a woman."

Klaus's face couldn't betray his shock and humiliation as Höss finalized the conversation by ordering Becker back to his post and personally escorting Veronika to the kitchen, where she would meet her new overlord.

Kapo Bronislaw Sinkowski was an obese Polish Jew with a gnarly pockmarked face that looked like igneous rock, with a lava rock soul to match. He was appointed to this position due to his fierce managerial skills, having been a banker, and his penchant for procurement. Bronislaw commandeered whatever he needed from local farmers to prepare the best private dinners for Höss, not to mention getting other luxuries like cases of cognac, schnapps and Höss's favorite Ibar cigarettes from Yugoslavia.

Höss escorted Veronika down the stone path alongside the kitchen. Her eyes veered up at the white clapboard-sided building with its twelve tall chimneys, each billowing feverishly. At the end of the building she could hear the orchestra playing a jovial tune in the courtyard. Yet the music was strained as an invisible nervousness filled the air, merging with the rancid smell emanating from the crematorium's overworked chimneys. For on the minds of everyone was the fate of millions, who sang to a different tune—one of unthinkable torture and gruesome death.

Arriving at the entrance they were stopped by Höss's adjutant, who had run up behind them to deliver important news. The commandant had an urgent telephone call; Himmler was on the line, waiting impatiently. Höss opened the kitchen door and instructed Veronika what to say and pointed to Sinkowski, who was on the far side of the kitchen, sitting at a table eating. Veronika nodded and anxiously entered while Höss and his adjutant departed.

Solemnly, Veronika approached Bronislaw and stood before him. His murky, yellow veiny-eyes dotted with brown, manure-like irises gazed up from the greasy chicken leg he was gnawing on to scan her body from head to toe. "You are very pretty and in good shape. And you will need to stay in good shape if you expect to survive here."

Veronika wiped away the small drip of blood on her lip with her finger. "I intend to stay in perfect good health, Kapo Sinkowski, and carry out whatever tasks you require. Particularly since the commandant informed me that the only way for me to keep my son Donato alive is for me to please you."

Veronika loathed saying those last three words as she felt they could be mistaken as being a proposition, yet they were the specific words Höss told her she must say.

Bronislaw's left brow rose, as his yellow lizard eyes widened. He had been instructed that anyone brought before him stating those three lovely words meant he had free license to not only physically abuse them but also engage in whatever sexual activities he wished without reprisals. Moreover, this gift code pertained not only to women, but also to young boys, a special delicacy of Kapo Sinkowski's.

Bronislaw licked his thick, meaty lips, which looked like two slabs of raw beef, and placed the now polished chicken bone down. He picked up a red cloth napkin featuring his monogram and began wiping his oily fingers. "That is most wise of you," he said as he then began picking his teeth with his unusually long fingernail. "What is your name?"

"Veronika Scalia."

"Ah, a rare Italian dish," he said as his fingernail continued burrowing between his teeth. "I'm glad you have your son's well-being as a motive to stay alive and the desire to satisfy me, because one woman, who was without child, made a foolish mistake. She dared to disobey me, thinking my threats idle." His baritone voice rose with emphasis. "Yet with the snap of my finger..." his chunky digits snapped "...her *heart* went idle!" His menacing eyes peered right through her fleshy orbs into the back of her skull. "Make no mistake, my little Mona Lisa, the commandant authorizes me to carry out whatever punishments I deem necessary." Inspecting his fingernail, Bronislaw then licked the small chicken debris off his pincer and wiped his salivary finger on his pant leg. He stood up. "Follow me."

Walking her through the kitchen, they passed several women dicing and slicing vegetables, a few men carving meat, and others cooking on stovetops or scuttling about cleaning or delivering food. Without turning his head, Bronislaw said, "These chefs are preparing dinner for the officers and guards, as good produce and meats cannot be wasted on prisoners."

"How do you do it?" Veronika asked.

"How do I do what? Manage this large enterprise?" Bronislaw asked as he continued to plod forward.

"No, how do you feed these German pigs who are murdering your fellow Jews while giving your own kind a smidgeon of stale bread and rancid water?"

Bronislaw stopped short as Veronika almost collided into him. Angrily, he spun around. "And are *you* deaf?"

Veronika's head jerked back, perplexed. "What do you mean?"

Bronislaw's rocky, pockmarked face rippled like boiling magma as he erupted, "I mean did you not hear the tale I just told of that foolish woman!? Do you doubt the extent of my powers as well?"

"K-Kapo Sinkowski," Veronika stammered, "of course I don't doubt your authority. My point is this, if you have such power, why not choose to help your people rather than add to their misery?"

With his hefty hand, Bronislaw forcefully grabbed Veronika by the nape of her neck. The kitchen staff briefly glanced their way knowing better to look the other way as they nervously resumed working. Meanwhile, Bronislaw dragged Veronika outside into the twilight as gray clouds began to obscure the sun.

The symbolism was apt as Veronika felt like the light in her life was being blotted out as well. She had been pressing her luck, dealing with one Nazi barbarian after another, and now being in the hands of a ruthless kapo with unfettered powers, she feared her lucky sevens had finally turned into snake eyes.

Bronislaw dragged her into a large shed with several goats and chicken coops. Locking the doors, he grabbed a long carving knife off the wall rack. Veronika's eyes widened as she stepped backwards, yet Bronislaw unexpectedly grabbed a goat, lobbed it on the table, and while it struggled to regain its balance he slit its throat! The animal squealed in agony as blood spurt from its arteries, splattering them both. In shock, Veronika covered her mouth, repulsed, as Bronislaw declared, "In this world, *I* am God! I can give or take life. Today, I sliced a goat's neck. Tomorrow, do I slice *yours?*"

Veronika's whole body shook as she tried to look into his evil eyes. Yet the gurgling sounds of the still suffering goat kept drawing her eyes to the poor helpless animal. "Why must you slit anyone's throat?" she nervously uttered.

"Because I can. And because you had better learn the ways of this new world we live in, or you will end up like this goat." With a rapid slash, Bronislaw then slit the goat's underbelly as its entrails fell on the table, the animal's legs giving way as it collapsed. "You may think I'm cruel, Veronika, but I am just wise enough to make the best out of this shitty world of ours. I'm a survivor, and my options as a Jew are to be either a pathetic cowering lamb, like all those I manage, or be the mighty lion, affording me to eat well, seize whatever pleasures I want, and live like King Herod, rather than suffer and die like your Christ. The meek, Veronika, will *never* inherit the Earth."

Veronika swallowed hard. "The meek may never inherit the Earth, Kapo Sinkowski, but they sure will inherit Heaven. So while you may savagely rule for a few years down here, aren't you concerned about eternity?"

Bronislaw snickered. "Look around you. Wake up! While some may have been criminals and deserved being executed, the vast majority are innocent men, women, and children. What crimes have they committed? None! So if this is how God brutally terrorizes and annihilates his *chosen* flock on Earth, it is pure folly to believe he will be merciful in the hereafter. And that's *if* you're foolish enough to still think he even exists." Wiping the goat's blood off the knife, he continued, "And having witnessed firsthand the brutality of the Nazis for several years now, as they savagely executed my whole family right before my eyes, and how invincible they are, by their lightning wars that continue to pulverize one nation after another, one can only say that every faith that man has created, from Ra and Mithras to Yahweh and Jesus have been pathetic delusions. Faith, Veronika, holds no key to survival here on Earth or for any vaporous childhood fantasy of a blissful eternity in Heaven."

Veronika's steadfast faith rose up, as she replied, "So, Kapo *Sin*-kowski, you prefer to sin and gamble on something you don't understand?" She wiped the goat's splattered blood off her face. "Mortals don't have the capacity to think on the elevated level of God. Only fools and belligerent villains think they do. That is what happens when people don't have the fear of God to temper them. It creates mayhem, fear, and even genocides, like what these self-imposed Aryan demigods are doing right now."

Bronislaw laughed. "I've heard all the religious mumbo jumbo before. It is fine for a select few—wearing impressive vestments and erecting awe-inspiring basilicas, temples and mosques—to instill fear in their flocks so they can control them, though, isn't it? It is easy for them to say God gave them their exalted mystical power, a power, no less, that none of them can ever truly perform on demand. No, no, Veronika, you have it all wrong. Charlatans rule the world, whether they wear a vestment, a suit, or a military uniform. They all deceive the masses to some extent, as human ambition is always fueled by self-interest. And while some of these religious charlatans may truly believe they were ordained for such a calling, their megalomania doesn't change reality; the charade prevails, a charade that has amazingly kept mankind shackled in ignorance for tens of thousands of years." Thrusting the carving knife into the goats hide, he continued, "But enough of this debate, as it is clear your blind allegiance is too deeply ingrained into your pretty little head. So, if reason cannot convince you, then perhaps some more visual and practical exercises in reality are necessary."

Bronislaw unlocked the shed doors and waved for her to exit. Reluctantly, Veronika passed slowly through the threshold as he briskly closed the doors and began walking beside her. Veronika was perspiring with anxiety as her eyes curiously scanned ahead. Spotlights lit up the camp as SS guards with machine guns kept a vigilant eye out for any signs of disturbance. A long line of men and teenaged boys were shuffling back to their barracks, their hunched backs and weary figures looking like browbeaten animals in a zoo being overworked and malnourished. Bronislaw smiled as he pointed to an SS guard holding back his snarling German Shepherd on a short leash. "Ah, there is Pearlie—a great animal trainer. You must watch this."

As Veronika turned, Pearlie uttered in the dog's ear, *"Töte ihn!"* and then unleashed the animal. The Shepherd lunged at a gaunt man too weak to walk and tore into his groin. The man screamed in agony as the dog's head shook in a violent frenzy, tearing off a chunk of the man's genitals. The frail man fell to the ground wailing as fellow inmates paused to gape at the horrific sight. The dog then attacked the prostrate man, biting and tearing at his neck for the final kill.

Veronika cringed and covered her eyes as Bronislaw gently removed her hands from her face. "You must get used to Auschwitz if you intend to survive, my dear. That man was weak—*useless*. Ever since 1939, with their T-4 program, the Nazis have been killing off their own useless citizens with mental illness and physical disabilities. The worthless only burden the strong. So, you see, if the German nation has been well groomed to accept the disposal of their own kind then surely eliminating subhuman Jews, Poles, Slavs or Soviets will not raise an eyebrow. This is simply the new order of things."

"Well, I prefer to think for myself," Veronika replied. "Following leaders that breed rabid dogs and sadistic humans is something I'm too intelligent and humane to ever embrace."

Bronislaw chuckled. "The words of a young idealist, I see. Utopia exists only in the minds of the weak. Yes, people too weak to face the truth." Bronislaw waved to a fellow kapo who was prodding another group of Jewish prisoners back to their barracks. Obediently, they shuffled in, one after the other, dressed in their drab gray clothes, with dour gray faces, and deadened gray souls. The sight was pitiable yet peculiar, as they appeared to be mere shadows of their former selves—emotionless, lifeless, almost too willing to accept their torturous state of despair and resignation.

Bronislaw gazed down at Veronika. "The transformation of my people is sickening. We Jews—once strong warriors that ruthlessly razed Canaan to the ground, killing every man, woman and child—had been beaten into submission by the indomitable Romans for being rebellious. Then for many centuries our browbeaten ancestors scattered to all points in Europe. Yet the jaundiced eyes of our new hosts prevented us from acquiring certain jobs, while their own silly religion frowned upon Christians taking on the role of banker, being damned as a usurer. As such, the plaques on many bankers' desks gradually changed from Reichart and Shultz to Rosen and Schwartz. The same held true among stockbrokers, lawyers, physicians, and newspapermen. Whereas the aristocratic Germans preferred to rest on their laurels or down a brew, the Jew studied hard to start anew. Hence, the Jews' egregious error, at least in the eyes of our overlords, was being successful…thus inciting jealousy and hatred. But in retrospect, it now appears our most harmful error was the shift from physical bull-work to civilized mental-work, thus turning courageous warriors into cowardly worms. And that, my dear, explains why my spineless, fellow Jews willingly shuffle themselves into the gas chambers and ovens like worthless invertebrates. It's mind-boggling! Pathetic! But that's the reality."

Veronika's weight shifted from one leg to the other as she pondered Bronislaw's philosophy, then replied, "Well, becoming civilized does tame the beast in some respects, but Attila the Hun didn't have deadly dive bombers or tanks, we do. So I would venture to say advancement might only be a partial explanation. But you overlooked a key factor in the persecution of Jews from the very start. Namely, their obstinate refusal to assimilate. Strict orthodox religions have their merits, but often times it's only within their cloistered communities. Being Italian, my father drilled in me the importance of researching our own past. The Romans have been vilified for centuries, yet despite their flaws, they had liberally offered to all their citizens and provinces the freedom to practice their own religion. But by many extant accounts, the Jews were treacherous and hostile. The curiously silenced texts by ancient Romans—as well as passages right in the New Testament or by the Jewish historian,

Josephus—reveal enlightening tales of the deadly intrigue and rampages inflicted upon the Romans by various Hebrew tribes. And those first stones that were cast precipitated the Empire's harsh reprisals, and explains why the Romans destroyed their Temple, inciting the large exodus you mentioned." As a beam of light swept across their faces from the guard tower above, Veronika squinted and continued, "So the exclusionary nature of the Jewish religion appears to be at the core of their troubles among the citizens of the world, and that's why my Jewish mother did the unthinkable, she abandoned what she felt was a faith born in bigotry to walk into the welcoming arms of Catholicism. Mind you, Christianity has its flaws, but its doctrine of tolerance appears to be why Christianity grew so rapidly and why the *chosen* rebuff of Judaism has been its perpetual undoing."

Bronislaw's lips twisted. "A somewhat sagacious rebuttal from such young woman, despite my preference to disagree, *studente*," he said with a condescending air.

Veronika looked up into his murky eyes as haggard prisoners and healthy guards sauntered past them in the oppressive darkness. "Don't get me wrong, Kapo, despite my mother's change of faith, I have many Jewish relatives and friends whom I love dearly, as I harbor no ill will toward any Jew, unless they give me cause to. But don't you think it's a bit odd how the Jews condemn the Aryans for their haughty racial snobbery, yet fail to see how their own religion likewise shuns the *unchosen*? There's a dark irony there, is there not?"

Bronislaw snorted. "The Aryan Superman versus The Chosen Jew is *no* contest in my mind. Despite my loss of faith, Jews believe in God, a higher being than themselves. Meanwhile, Aryans believe in Hitler and Himmler's haughty heap of horseshit! It's utter nonsense that a child of three could easily dispute; yet the pathetic Germans revel in their self-exultation like moronic cavemen goose-stepping around a campfire that's sizzling with human flesh and burnt books." With an upturned nose, he added, "So your feeble attempt to persuade me, my dear, has gone up in smoke!"

"Well, naturally I agree that the concept of the Aryan super-race is ludicrous," Veronika replied, "however, all I'm saying is, look at Judaism from another perspective. Not only diehard Nazis, but millions of Buddhists, Shinto, Hindus and others across the globe view the Jewish God as a fictitious myth, one who is vengeful, jealous, and has catastrophic tantrums worse than Zeus. Despite your outward denial of God, your ingrained Jewish faith still holds sway in your mind. But others see it differently. In their minds, Aryanism and Judaism are both troublesome cults with similar traits. Where Moses annihilated the Canaanites, Hitler plans to annihilate the Jews. Therefore, if we briefly distance ourselves from the religious teachings of our youth, we too could see how they both share underlying prejudices. Wouldn't you agree?"

Bronislaw rolled his eyes, not appreciating having his petite, pretty pupil lecture *him*, especially since she was cleverly using the ancient philosophers' device of ending her provocative rebuttals with a question. "Well, I think it is time to *distance ourselves* from this conversation." With a grunt, he said, "Now move! This way."

Bronislaw and Veronika walked along the kitchen building and past the entrance gate, with its deceptive slogan "Work Brings Freedom." Meanwhile, sounds of Richard Strauss's *Symphonia Domestica* filled the evening air with a pleasant sound (depicting the composer's joyous family life) as the orchestra in the courtyard played, once again attempting to deceive the inmates that a normal domestic life somehow existed in Hell.

Veronika rolled her eyes, repulsed, as Bronislaw declared, "You see, as I've told you—the world is orchestrated by masterful conductors of illusions."

Veronika squinted. "Interesting analogy. But I believe you mean by masterful *composers*," she corrected.

"No, no," he replied with a professorial air, reaffirming his eminent stature. "Although the conductor is nowhere near as brilliant or creative as the composer, it is the conductor who utilizes the knowledge of others to command the spotlight and enrapture his audience with dramatic gestures and charisma, just like politicians, popes and rabbis. So, you see, my dear, you are obviously either too young or too gullible to decipher the true mechanics of illusion."

As they continued their nocturnal journey, Bronislaw persisted with his intense lecture. "My initial intention, Veronika, was to have you slaughter livestock. But killing animals is simply part of human existence. You see, before I was a banker I had been a doctor, actually a veterinarian. I grew up on a farm, and even as a young boy, it was I whom farmers relied upon to ensure their livestock remained healthy. Until, that is, the day their animals were brutally slaughtered. As a boy this gruesome act seemed exceedingly cruel to me. Sure, people needed to eat, but to mislead those poor animals by caring for them, some of which I had grown very fond of, only to kill them, was profoundly disturbing. Oddly enough, however, after some time, having matured and reading voraciously, reality set in. What had once been emotionally upsetting had become logically edifying. In a nutshell, Veronika, only the strong survive." Passing a guard, Bronislaw smiled and gave him a thumbs-up as the guard nodded with a grin. Turning back toward Veronika, he added, "So I have learned to transfer that knowledge from the animal world to human nature. After all, we're all just animals that live, breathe, bleed, and die, so it's childish to pretend otherwise."

Under the cloud-filled, starless night sky they approached their destination as Bronislaw pointed to a redbrick building some ten yards away. Veronika's eyes widened as she gasped. She knew very well this was the infamous Little Red House. Stunned with terror, she watched a sprawling mass of mothers and their children, along with several frail old men, cascade past her. Their shadowy gaunt faces, eerily lit by electric lampposts and the moonlight above, added to the chilling specter of impending doom.

SS guards and SS *Helferinnen* were calmly cajoling the crowd, utilizing the commandant's new lulling protocol, leading them to an area partially obstructed by a thick network of branches. Once there, Veronika heard one *Helferin* say loudly, "Ladies, please undress yourselves and your children. Keep all your clothes and any belongings in a neat pile. You may collect them after delousing." As the women nervously gazed at each other and began disrobing, an *Unterführer* reassured them of the normalcy of their cleansing process by pointing to a pile of clean towels.

Veronika stood emotionally paralyzed a short distance away as Bronislaw stood beside her, delighting in his lesson of cruel reality. She ventured to look away, but was reminded of the deadly price she'd pay for disobedience.

As she struggled to keep her eyes open, a mass of over two hundred naked women, children, and old men were being escorted toward the entrance doors. Their emaciated, skeletal bodies, deprived of food, and now humiliatingly subjected to family, friends, and foe only exacerbated the crime as some guards made cruel jokes, while others tried to mollify the human cattle before the slaughter.

Meanwhile a four-year-old naked little girl was straying from the crowd when a *Helferin* grabbed her hand and picked her up. The tiny girl flinched, startled by the stranger, but then smiled, revealing her dimples and teeny rice-like teeth. The *Helferin* flashed a motherly smile and began tickling the child, making her giggle, then placed her back into the production line of death, patting her bare little bottom with a beguiling wink.

As the shadowy procession passed, a mother carrying her infant son glanced deeply into Veronika's eyes, the light from above illuminating the woman's harried face and amplifying her searing optical plea for salvation. The human connection was too much to bear, and Veronika closed her eyes tight, the excruciating pain crushing her heart as sympathy oozed from every pore in her body.

Unexpectedly, Veronika twitched. Bronislaw had clutched her arm. Gazing up into his yellow beastly eyes, Veronika was repulsed—not only by his ugly face, which now sported a morbid grin of satisfaction, but also by his cold granite heart that had acclimated to condoning this ungodly deed.

Two SS guards then dutifully closed the doors and began locking them. Veronika's body quaked, the horror and urge to intervene rapidly mounting inside her like a swarm of killer bees, when suddenly flashes of Donato filled her mind.

Bronislaw was quick to recognize the tumult of indecision that now raged inside her and acted promptly. "I know what you're thinking, Veronika. But you would be dead before you ever managed to open those doors. Moreover, let me add this addendum to my threat: not only would Donato be killed, but so, too, would ten random comrades of yours from your barracks who were not even selected for extermination."

Veronika's eyes rolled up at the beast. "Again, I must ask, how can you do such evil things and sleep at night?"

"I sleep fine, my pretty little protégé, as will these prisoners. Yet, their slumbers will deliver them to your sweet heavenly paradise. After all, isn't *that* the fairyland you firmly believe in. So why worry your pretty little face, Veronika? Condition your mind. They will soon leave all this misery behind as their work here *has* set them free." His antagonistic grin turned dead serious. "Now follow me!"

As they walked alongside the makeshift death-chamber, Veronika glanced up. The eerie, windowless expanse of the redbricked wall, with its crudely bricked-in windows, was even visually suffocating. Reaching the rear of the Little Red House, they turned the corner. Standing before them in the shadowy recesses of night stood two guards, each holding a round tin canister. At first surprised by the unexpected visit, the guards soon nodded their approval, confirming the kapo's distinct features.

Then the horror struck as Bronislaw instructed one of the guards, "*Sturmmann*, give this woman the canister."

Veronika gasped and shrieked. *"No!* Please! You can't make me do this!"

Bronislaw signaled the guard with a nod, and gazed back at Veronika. "This is all part of the lesson, Veronika. I *will* drill reality into you, one way or another. *Now take it!"* he commanded.

The SS guard pulled out his Luger and pointed it at her head. Extending his hand with the canister, he instructed, "Take it. *Quickly*. The prisoners will get suspicious if we delay much longer."

Veronika's heart dropped as she hesitantly grasped the tin canister. Her eyes drifted down as moonlight illuminated the label. She spun the cylinder slowly. The chilling letters of death read "Zyklon-B: Made in Hamburg."

Her eyes darted back up at Bronislaw and again she pleaded, but the guard shoved the pistol to her temple and barked, *"Mach schnell!"*

The other guard had already reached up to the hole in the brick wall, and now waited for Veronika; their doses had to be synchronized. Tears welled in Veronika's eyes as she was pushed to the other hole. She could hear the muffled voices of the prisoners inside; some reciting the *Shema Yisrael* prayer with trembling voices, and mothers trying to mollify their frightened children, as one cried out, "Mummy, Mummy, hold me! I'm scared."

Veronika suddenly felt a crack on the back of her head. Bronislaw had taken the SS guard's Luger and battered her as he now barked, "Open the canister, Veronika, and pour it in. *Now!"*

She hesitated, the weight of indecision clouding her mind as the horrific consequences of if she does or doesn't comply teetered on the scale. Removing the lid, she glanced at the other guard, who nodded and then poured in his canister. Veronika closed her eyes, and with the barrel of Bronislaw's pistol pushed against her occipital bone, she tipped her hand as death flowed.

Within seconds a violent flurry of bone-chilling screams radiated out of the building, sending a wretched chill throughout Veronika's body. Keeling over with nausea, tears streamed down her cheeks as she gazed up to face the Devil. "I will *never* forgive you for this. Somehow, someway, I *will* make you pay for this."

Bronislaw smiled as the harrowing cries of panic-stricken prisoners filled the night air. Veronika vomited and broke down, weeping inconsolably. To her further dismay, the frenzied scratching, wailing and choking continued for ten excruciating minutes.

Veronika fell to the ground, leaning against the brick building with her face buried in her hands. Visions of the mothers and their adorable children flashed in her mind's eye, along with the old men who had shuffled past her into the chamber, emaciated by starvation and half dead already. She realized now that she never should have looked at any of them as they passed her, as their innocent, terrified or unknowing faces were now burnt into her memory, never to be forgotten.

For a half hour, Veronika sat numb and disengaged from the horrid world around her as her once luminous soul sank into a hellish black pit of unbearable anguish.

Awaking from the sounds of boots hitting dirt and metal wheels clanking over gravel, Veronika gazed up to see a unit of Slavic and Ukrainian commandos unlock the doors.

These hardened ex-cons, who had avoided a death sentence, now had the grueling task of cadaver disposal. Having waited the prescribed half-hour interval to allow the poison gas to dissipate, they now entered the chambers like scavenging vultures. Rummaging through the heaping mounds of dead bodies they began prying open their mouths searching for gold teeth. Those who literally struck gold pulled out a knife and carved the teeth out, while others stripped the dead of their wedding bands, earrings or any jewelry they wore or hid in orifices.

Veronika looked away, but was once again forced to watch the horrific sight as Bronislaw stood above her, emotionless, with the Luger still clutched in his hand.

Having collected all the valuables, the commandos then placed them in a large bin. They would later be melted down and sent to Berlin. In essence, the Jews were supplying the Nazi war machine with millions in Reichsmarks to fund their own extinction and Hitler's quest to conquer the world. Now, however, began the next phase, as the commandos began tossing the limp bodies into lorries. As they did, the bodies bounced like hard rubber while the arms and legs flapped haphazardly. Veronika cringed. The sight was profoundly disturbing. These once warm-blooded, animated human beings had been chillingly reduced into inert, rubber-like manikins. Her mind went numb, struggling to process insanity.

With the main camp's incinerators deactivated, since they had been inconveniently located next to the barracks, the commandos now had to cart the bodies out to a field where a large ditch had been dug. Hauling the cadavers into the pit, they then inserted firewood between them as kindling. Veronika attempted to look away, but Bronislaw nudged her with the pistol. Through tears of bloodshot eyes, Veronika gazed over the vast expanse of carnage. It was grotesque, surreal, unreal. Dazed and queasy, she watched the commandos take rags soaked with paraffin and ignite the mass funeral pyre. As the flames roared and flesh began to burn, the stench was unbearable. The ungodly smell aptly mirrored the nauseating sight before her as the sinful glow of hundreds of bodies being cremated reflected in her eyes. Veronika could feel the intense heat as it warmed her face and the front of her body, while inside, her heart burned with pity for all the innocent souls subjected to such a merciless and ignoble fate.

Bronislaw remained emotionless as he gazed deep into the blazing fire. Without turning, he said, "I spared you, Veronika, from joining the commandos in carrying out these laborious tasks, not because you're a woman—for tomorrow you *will* join them—but because of a childhood experience I had that I now realize has come full circle." Turning to face Veronika, he continued, "As a young boy I had disobeyed my father, who only allowed my brother and me to read the Torah, the only book, mind you, in our farmhouse. Having a will of my own, I was compelled to follow my curiosity and seek the writings of authors from different cultures and even conflicting religions. As such, Dante's *Divine Comedy* had enthralled me, and I read the *Inferno* with great fascination. And like Virgil escorting Dante through the Circles of Hell, I have thus escorted you, my Italian wanderer, through Hell on Earth."

A sinister smile etched Bronislaw face, delighted with his hellish tale.

As the fire roared and crackled, Veronika replied strategically, "Well, Bronislaw, to remain faithful to Dante's allegory, you have shown me Hell, but after Purgatory you must allow Beatrice to escort me to Paradise."

Bronislaw laughed disdainfully. "Ha! Very clever, *mia bella studente*. But you have made two very crucial mistakes. First, I am *not faithful* to *anything*, except my own survival. And second, there is no Beatrice or knight in shining armor that can save you. This Hell and Purgatory has no Gate to Paradise. So to quote Dante's fitting words to the *Inferno*, 'Abandon all hope ye who enter here!'"

Veronika's head dropped as her hopes plummeted into a dark cavernous pit nine layers deep.

Momentarily lost in a sullen fog, Veronika was jolted awake when Bronislaw needled her with the barrel of his gun. "Walk that way," he commanded as he pointed to a large cement slab surrounded by prisoners.

Veronika looked over. The prisoners were huddled around the huge block, apparently working on something, but what it was, she couldn't tell. As she and Bronislaw approached, her eyebrows pinched in confusion, managing to see only large piles of gray dust. Yet as they got closer, the morbid vision became manifest. There, before her eyes, were splintery shards of human bones protruding out of the ashes. Broken pieces of jawbones with jagged rows of teeth stood beside various fragments of skulls, pelvises and femurs. Working like coal miners pummeling anthracite, the prisoners pulverized the bones with wooden hammers.

Bronislaw handed Veronika a hammer. "These remains are from the previous cremation, as the pyre we just left will take six or seven hours to fully disintegrate the bodies. I expect you to crush these bones until the dawn, at which time I will return to collect you." Glancing briefly back at the SS guards armed with machineguns, he added, "And know that your every move will be carefully monitored. So get cracking!"

Twilight had quickly turned to night, yet dusk's journey to dawn dragged on and on as Veronika pulverized bone after bone and skull after skull. With aching wrists and heavy eyelids, her horrible task, which started out as a gruesome desecration of the dead, turned into a grueling and monotonous physical chore. Her tired mind began contemplating the hell she'll be forced to face again tomorrow, when tears, once again, welled in her eyes. Hours passed when the faint glimmer of dawn touched the horizon, yet Veronika was still lost inside her dark cerebral dungeon. The disturbing thought of having poured the Zyklon-B into the chamber sent chills through her body. *Should I have taken the bullet?* she questioned. *Then again, after Bronislaw would have shot me he would have poured the poison himself. So all those poor souls would have been murdered anyhow, as well as Donato and ten people from my barracks. My sacrifice would have actually increased the death toll. Dear God. Please! I beg you, tell me what I must do to get out of this Hell?*

Shattering her mental plea was the surprise return of Bronislaw, as his baritone voice bellowed, "I see you had a productive night." He ran his fingers through the pile of ashes, lifting up a handful and then spreading his fingers as microscopic particles of people sifted through falling to the ground. Veronika was too tired to even excoriate the beast who had no respect for the dead or the living.

He then looked at her with a creepy smile. "My, you are a beautiful woman, Veronika. In fact, it would be a pity to shave all that gorgeous hair off of you. The Nazis have certainly collected enough hair from prisoners to stuff millions of pillows and mattresses for the Reich, so, as a special bonus, you may keep yours. Actually, I loathe looking at all these bald women around here. The ugly ones, who cares, they're beasts anyhow, but the cute little darlings, like you, need hair to please *me*." He chuckled. "So, the bonus is not really for you." He turned and pointed.

Commandos were shoveling the ashes into large bins, as he said, "They will now take these ashes and dump them in the Vistula River. Their journey will soon be over, yet yours has just begun." He pointed to a large hut. "So get some daytime rest in your new accursed abode and I will wake you to start this process all over again at twilight."

Veronika's new barrack was a ramshackle hut packed tight with prisoners, dilapidated three-tiered bunks with four people crammed per tier, and infested with lice. Weeks passed, and then to Veronika's horror, months passed, and still no sign from above as to how to escape Bronislaw's infernal nightmare. The only consolation Veronika had was that Bronislaw never asked her again to pour the poison. However, her grueling tasks to assist the commandos in hauling the dead bodies, removing their jewelry and gold teeth, and pulverizing the bones had taken its toll. Her body ached, her stomach cried out for more food than just stale bread and water, and her mind was drifting in and out of a traumatized state of hallucinations.

It was now July 20, 1942, and Veronika was wearily standing at the slab of ashes and bones, scratching her lice-bitten head, when she smashed a jawbone. Several teeth shot upward in scattered directions, one hitting Bronislaw in the face as he approached. "Watch what the hell you're doing!" he blasted as he rubbed the blemish. "Put the hammer down. I must impart some very important news." As Veronika complied, Bronislaw continued, "Heinrich Himmler had visited the camp yesterday. His instructions to Commandant Höss were that the executions must be intensified. The entire Jewish population in the General Government must be exterminated by December 31."

"*Dear God,*" Veronika retorted, now jarred awake. "Will their madness ever cease?" Overwhelmed by the horrifying news, however, a stream of tears trickled down her cheeks. Her shoulders dropped and her back hunched over as she wiped the tears away leaving a smear of human dust on her face. "I don't know how much more of this I can take."

Bronislaw's granite face cracked with a smile of satisfaction as he reached over and placed his hefty hand on her shoulder. "Well, there is some good news in all of this, Veronika...for *you* that is."

Veronika recoiled as she glanced at his unwanted hand and uncomfortably stepped back.

Bronislaw's hand fell back by his side as he said, "Well, Veronika, with a greater influx of healthy prisoners, I could very well appoint a new arrival to take your place, *if* you are willing to be my personal secretary."

Veronika looked up into Bronislaw's murky brown and yellow eyes, which now seemed to have an unusual glow. "Why are you making this offer now? And just what would you expect of me as your secretary?"

"Well, now that my disobedient secretary was sent to the chamber, I'm in need of a replacement. And since I have finally broken your foolish will I believe you are now ready to face reality. Naturally, I'll expect you to carry out whatever demands I ask."

Veronika couldn't restrain her face from broadcasting revulsion, which Bronislaw glumly received loud and clear. Promptly, he took remedial action. "Now be reasonable, Veronika. Think about it. You will never have to haul, strip, or mash any more dead prisoners. In fact, you will never have to even witness these exterminations ever again, as I will give you new clothes, silk stockings, a real bed and bathtub, a delicious selection of our finest foods, and—"

"Orders to pleasure you," Veronika retorted.

Bronislaw laughed, his pockmarked face and fat lips rippling in unison with every jiggle of his blubbery belly. "You make that sound worse than your revolting mortuary tasks right now, not to mention the physical and psychological abuses you have tried to endure. Unsuccessfully, may I add."

"I'm still standing," Veronika said as she struggled to stay erect. Yet her overwrought body and mind, coupled with the pathetically small rations she had been allotted, had worn her down, just as Bronislaw had planned.

"Yes, Veronika, you're still standing, but just barely. You had just wept and admitted that you didn't know how much more of this you could take. So, *take* my offer. I am your only salvation. This you must have learned by now."

Veronika swayed, her vision blurry, and her tired and tortured mind trying to process Mephistopheles's offer.

"Very well," Bronislaw said calmly, "then perhaps I might as well tell you. Donato was exterminated yesterday, orders of Klaus Becker."

Her ashen fingers dug into her cheeks as she wailed. "Oh God, *No! No!*" Her legs gave way, her body falling onto her knees as she hunched over and wept bitterly.

"So you see, Veronika, there's no reason for you to suffer here with the dead, or with these Polish and Slavic grunts with dysentery, scarlet fever, and lice. Come with me, and this hell will all end."

Veronika shook her head and continued to weep.

Bronislaw's lips twisted in frustration. He was intent on breaking her will and had used up all his evil cards, but now it was time to finally pull out his deadly ace, as he said, "Very well, my dear, then tomorrow you will resume the task of administering Zyklon-B."

He turned and began walking away as Veronika's eyes sprang open. Frightened with desperation, she wobbled up to her feet and struggled to catch him, just barely managing to grab his arm as her weak body lurched. Bronislaw turned and clutched her elbow to steady her as she fell into his arms. "*No!* Please!" she cried, "I can never do that again. *Never!* I will do whatever you wish, but no more death. I can't bear it another day."

Gratification reeked from Bronislaw's pores as he lifted her frail body up and looked into her still beautiful eyes. "I'll have you know, my dear, that my name, Bronislaw, means 'Protector of Glory.' So you have literally fallen into the hands that will protect you, Veronika, from now on. All you need to do now is refocus your will to live. To quote Nietzsche: 'He who has a Why to live for can bear almost any How.' And you have finally learned Why it is wise to live for *me*—your protector and savior."

Grasping her elbow and shoulder firmly, Bronislaw smiled as he began escorting his long-awaited trophy back to his barrack.

7

The Visitor

Veronika dreamily awoke the next morning to *A Midsummer Night's Dream*. She truly wasn't certain if she was awake or dreaming, but the pleasant music drew her eyes to the gramophone in the corner of the room. Her eyes then slowly scanned the room to see the cheerful light-blue painted walls, windows with curtains, and the smell of eggs and bacon wafting through the pure air. The beautiful vision was broken, however, when Kapo Sinkowski's ugly face appeared before her.

"How do you like your eggs?" he said with an awkward smile.

Veronika rubbed the sleep away from her eyes as the new horror of what she had bargained for with the Devil came screaming into her mind. Anxiously, she answered, "Uh, I suppose…scrambled is fine."

Bronislaw tried to exude charm as best he could, but it was like a wild smelly boar covered in mud striving to be a debonair penguin donning a tux.

"I hope you like my choice of music?"

"Yes," she said softly, "its by Felix Mendelssohn."

"Correct," Bronislaw replied. "It is not easy to get recordings of Jewish composers in Nazi Germany."

Veronika sat upright. "I imagine it wouldn't."

Bronislaw wiped the sweat away from his pocked face, the July heat and humidity punishing his massive body. "I know you still must have doubts about me, Veronika, but I am a very successful and cultured man. I have always maintained financial security through the Twenties and the depression. Even here in hell I've managed to live like a king, while others slave in factories or perish. And once this war is over, I can provide you with a very comfortable life. In fact, tonight we will have a candlelit dinner and attend a concert at the camp theater. How does that sound?"

Veronika's heart dropped. "It sounds like the damnation of Faust."

Bronislaw's face twisted in anger at the insult, but then he chuckled. "Ah! Yes, of course. So you know what is on the program tonight. Berlioz's *Damnation of Faust* is a rather odd work, but quite enjoyable."

Veronika had indeed seen the poster announcing the concert, but she meant what she said. She knew she had made an ugly pact with Mephistopheles and, like Faust, would now suffer the consequences. Her life was damned. She closed her eyes, this time longer, contemplating the next circle of hell she would now have to endure.

"What's wrong?" Bronislaw queried. "Are you still fatigued?"

She had to delay this new circle of hell somehow, and she opened her eyes. "Yes, but it is more than just being tired, Bronislaw. It will take me several weeks to regain my strength back. I'm drained—physically and emotionally."

Bronislaw's apprehension turned into a smile. "Oh! Yes of course. By all means, relax." He had expected a flat-out rejection, but now his ego and libido were stoked. "You just stay in bed and convalesce, Veronika. Your health now means everything to me." He turned and stuck his large sweaty head out the open window then drew it back in. "Please excuse me, I must get our eggs and bacon. The commandant doesn't appreciate when I use a portable grill outside my barrack, the smell carries and entices—or rather antagonizes—the starving prisoners."

As he hobbled out the room, Veronika rose and dashed to the window. Peering out, she saw Bronislaw approach the grill and start flipping bacon as the sweat on his nose dripped into the frying pan. Repulsed by every fiber of his sweaty body, Veronika's mind raced as she turned and scanned the room. She just had to find something, anything at all that could end this nightmare. Her eyes landed on a pair of scissors. *No,* she thought, that blatant tactic would only land her in front of a firing squad. Just then the door opened.

Bronislaw strolled in with a plate of scrambled eggs and bacon. His head recoiled. "I thought you were exhausted and unwell?"

Veronika's stunned face went pale, and she swiftly used that to her advantage. "Actually, I just wanted to smell the food. I'm famished." She wiped her now sweaty forehead, and added, "I feel a bit flush and lightheaded. I might be running a fever."

Suspicion still took top billing in Bronislaw's mind as he placed the plate on the table. The July heat and grilling was getting overbearing and he peeled off his shirt. The rolls of fat, covered with a thick layer of sweaty black hair, caused Veronika to quiver. She attempted to conceal her revulsion, but couldn't as Bronislaw approached her.

As the "Nocturne" from *A Midsummer Night's Dream* played in the background, Bronislaw placed his hand on her forehead. "Hmm, it seems fine to me. No fever. No fever at all." His rough, meaty hand moved down to her shoulder then cascaded gently to her bicep. He *grabbed* it firmly. He yanked her into his clammy chest as Veronika's forearms pressed deep into his sweaty belly, her face being only centimeters away from his rank and hairy pectorals. "You seem fine to me, Veronika, my dear." He backed her up toward the bed as Veronika kicked and struggled to no avail. He then pushed her backward as she landed flat on her back on the bed. He unzipped his pants and unleashed his manhood as Veronika's petrified eyes widened. "No! You can't do this. Please!"

"The deal was you shall do whatever I ask, Veronika." Bronislaw's face contorted with anger. "Do you want to go back to the death chambers? We are now processing two thousand exterminations a day. Do you really think you'll last more than one day yourself?"

Veronika shimmied herself backward, her shoulders now pressed against the wall. "No, I can't go back. But I can't do this either." She had to placate him somehow and added, "I just need more time. That's all. I'm not ready—"

Just then the door swung open as a fifteen-year-old boy with bright red hair waltzed in. He stopped suddenly, his smile turned upside down, along with his now shattered life. His jaw dropped as he gazed at his lover standing half naked over a woman. Tears welled in his eyes as he spun around and darted out the door.

"Shit!" Bronislaw barked. "Goddamn it, Adam. Come back here!"

Zippering his pants, Bronislaw's face turned red. Veronika squinted, but decided to remain mute. Meanwhile, Bronislaw slipped on his shirt and began buttoning it. His stubby fingers then ran through his greasy hair like a comb as he gazed at Veronika, his embarrassment replaced with arrogance. "What's that look for? You must know that a man of my caliber does whatever he chooses. Besides, the Greeks built a whole civilization based upon ephebophilia." He swaggered to the door and spun around. "You stay put. A foolish attempt to stray will only get you killed. You *will* be mine, so ready yourself, *quickly!* I shall return." With that, he exited and slammed the door.

Veronika's face fell into the palms of her hands as the "Wedding March" from Mendelssohn's *A Midsummer Night's Dream* began playing on the gramophone. Veronika took her shoe and threw it, the mocking march being terminated.

Her lips rippled in frustration when, unexpectedly, the door swung open! Bronislaw stormed back into the room and slammed the door. Veronika froze as Bronislaw briefly turned to lock the door. "That petulant adolescent ran too damned fast for me," he huffed as he spun around, looking at Veronika with lustful eyes. "Adam is just a plaything to service me. Yet *he*, on the other hand, has taken on to me like a cock-sucking leech."

Veronika shook her head. "That's a callous way to speak of him. He obviously loves you."

Bronislaw laughed, his lardy stomach bouncing with each gust of rancid air that emanated from his vile mouth. "That queer little pipel is just one of many who service my needs. I *never* service theirs. I am not a homosexual, Veronika. It is just their mouths that interest me, and mouths are to be found on any human being, be it a boy, girl, man or woman."

Veronika closed her eyes, repulsed, while Bronislaw suddenly noticed the lopsided gramophone out of the corner of his eye. Turning his head, his eyes then cascaded to the tabletop beside it, where the record now sat, along with

Veronika's shoe. His face twitched with irritation as he walked over and picked up the disc, his eyes intently inspecting the damages. "This is a treasured recording by Deutsche Grammophon. Why would you do this?"

Veronika remained silent, but couldn't control her outright look of disgust as Bronislaw continued, "I'll have you know, for forty-four years Deutsche Grammophon had many great musicians signed, including my Uncle Solomon, who was an oboist in Leipzig. He in fact played on this recording." Bronislaw lovingly spun the record over as a lump welled in his throat. "But then in 1933, the world changed. That's when that deranged, Aryan upstart rose to power." Bronislaw pensively rubbed the hairline cracks in the brittle shellac disc with his finger. "Many of those musicians, like my uncle, were Jews and had to flee the country. The company began to falter steadily and, just recently, Siemens & Halske purchased it." Bronislaw's face twisted with a snarl. "But get this: they built a factory right *here* in Auschwitz. So now my uncle and many of his talented friends, who either stayed in Germany or fled to countries consumed by the Third Reich, are forced to be slave laborers. The sheer *gall* of it all!" Bronislaw's eyes oscillated, the reminder of the hell they all were subjected to only exacerbating his fury as he violently snapped the damaged record!

Veronika twitched. "I'm s-sorry about your record and your uncle. But if the company is right here in Auschwitz, why don't you simply replace it?"

Bronislaw's eyes glowed with venom. "There are things even *I* cannot do here. And never mind replacing the damn record. I think it's time to replace *you*," he spat. "But not before I get some satisfaction." He tossed the broken record on the floor and ripped off his shirt, the buttons popping off like popcorn. He then began undoing his belt as he plodded toward her. Veronika recoiled and eyed the small pole lamp near the bed.

Now fully naked, except for his black socks, Bronislaw kneeled on the edge of the bed and began crawling toward her. The bed buckled and creaked from his massive weight while his fat sweaty body jiggled with each knee-crawling stride. As he loomed before her, Veronika grabbed the lamp and smashed him across the face, the cracked bulb gouging a deep bloody ravine in his fleshy cheek. Bronislaw screamed in agony and grabbed his bleeding face, when, unexpectedly, someone's fist pounded the door, *repeatedly.*

Bronislaw irritably swiveled his head sideways, his eyes darting back toward the door. "Adam, go away!"

Veronika yelled, "Help me! Please!"

Bronislaw turned back toward his prey and grabbed her neck with one hand and covered her mouth with the other. His bloody face contorted like red-hot molten lava as his hefty hand began strangling her frail neck. Just then the door burst open by a hard kick and a commanding voice yelled, "Halt! Or I'll shoot!"

Bronislaw spun around while continuing to crush Veronika's larynx, his face stern and defiant. Veronika's eyes bulged, not only from Bronislaw's death grip, but also because of the apparition standing in the doorway.

I barked, "Let her go—*now!*" as I drew and aimed my Luger straight at the fat bastard's ugly head.

His demonic eyes widened with dread as he quickly released her. Veronika rubbed her bruised neck and croaked one word. "Jack!?"

Her face reeked of bafflement as I stepped fully into the room wearing my impressive *Oberführer der Waffen-SS* black uniform. It wasn't easy for me to do, but I had to do it. In perfect German I commanded, "Silence, bitch!" My eyes veered back to the repulsive hairy hippo on the bed. *"You,*

Kapo Sinkowski, get the fuck off the bed, and get dressed. *Now!"*

Bronislaw frantically fumbled with his clothing while Veronika retorted, "Bitch? How dare you! And what are you doing in—"

"Quiet!" I barked as I swiveled my gun, now pointing it at *her*. Meanwhile, two SS guards filed into the room behind me as I commanded, "Take this insolent bitch to my car. I'll teach her how we Germans deal with Soviet Jews."

Veronika gasped with shock and confusion as they grabbed her arms. Gazing at me with loathing in her eyes, she spat, "You were a damn Nazi all along!" The wheels in her head were clearly in high gear as she deduced her new reality. "That's why you told Hans Schmidt he would be sorry, and that explains how you evaded being tortured by that creep! Did he know all along? Or did you convince him of your highfalutin *SS Oberführer* rank?"

With my false straight-face clipped on tight, I said, "I'm glad you like to talk so much, because, before I kill you, there is much valuable information I need to extract from you...*Night Witch."*

As the SS guards smiled and began dragging her out, she turned her head to gaze back at me. "And for four months I mourned, thinking you were brutally tortured and killed. Now I wish you were!"

With her last dagger hurled into my heart, the guards escorted her to my staff car.

Heatedly, I turned around; it was time to finalize my dealings with the repulsive pig. Bronislaw was still buttoning his shirt as I said, "You better learn how to treat a lady, you fat piece of shit!" I then smashed his shocked ugly face, which snapped sideways. The swine's fat cheeks rippled as blood spurt out of his ripped, pork-chop lips.

He whipped his head back toward me, wiping his mutilated face, thanks also to Veronika's fine handiwork.

"Who are you?" he retorted, breathing heavily, like a pissed-off bull, while his fists shook with agitation at his sides. "Commandant Höss allows me any such pleasures I seek."

"Are you dense as well as depraved, Kapo!?" I barked, "Look at my insignia. Höss takes orders from *me*." As the cocky bull wilted back into a passive pig, I continued, "And the only pleasures you'll seek from now on will be to breathe and eat real food again. You are being thrown back into the pool of prisoners."

Bronislaw gasped, as he stammered, "Y-you can't do that t-to me. I'm a kapo! The prisoners would beat me to a pulp."

"That's the idea," I retorted. While I summoned a guard, I gazed at all his possessions. "Ah! That's a very nice Electrola gramophone."

"Take it!" Bronislaw pleaded. "I'll gladly give it to you, just spare me."

"It's already mine. And spare you? Ha! You're lucky I don't spear you."

The young guard marched in and stomped his feet. "Heil Hitler!" he barked enthusiastically, thrusting his hand upward.

With a passive flip of my hand, I returned the asinine salute and instructed him to escort the swine to Höss's office for standard processing. Tears welled in Bronislaw's eyes as the guard pushed him out of the room. I grasped *my* gramophone and walked back to my Kfz. 21 staff car. Veronika was sitting in the rear seat, with her hands shackled, while a storm trooper manned the steering wheel. I shoved the gramophone into the passenger's seat then slipped into the rear seat, next to the snarling lioness. As I turned to look at her, the constricted cat clawed me with her clasped hands across my face.

"Ouch!" I yelped as the metal shackle bruised my cheek.

The driver spun around and reached for his holster.

"No, no! It's fine." I commanded as I now looked at Veronika. "You *are* finished venting, correct?"

She just sat and grumbled, her heart racing and jaw clenched tight.

The driver looked at me. "I apologize, *meine Oberführer*, I should have shackled her to the arm rest."

"That won't be necessary, Fritz. Let's just get out of here. This place gives me the creeps."

As the staff car pulled away, Veronika shifted her body away from me, wedging herself up against the door. The loathing on her face was priceless as she spat, "Gives you the creeps!? You despicable coward! You can murder Jews, Poles, and Soviets by the thousands but you can't stomach watching it. And that includes children, many of them thrown into a pit and buried alive to save time or bullets, while some deranged guards toss babies into the air for target practice. It's nauseating! Grotesque! Barbaric! You Nazis are nothing but a virus to humanity."

"What are you talking about?" I said as our car gained velocity and the dreaded camp receded behind us. "It's a labor camp. I know they work a few people to death in the factories, and abuse others, but savage mass murder?"

As our car crossed over the railroad tracks, heading west, Veronika pointed north with her cuffed hands. "Look there! That's Auschwitz II – Birkenau. Do mean to say you're unaware of what you're doing in that slaughterhouse?"

I turned and gazed northward. In the distance I saw a huge sprawling complex of single-story buildings, built of the same rough, redbrick as the main camp. Near the center, a two-story tower, with a row of windows wrapped around the top, had an arched entranceway where a railroad track ran straight into the complex. A locomotive, with a seemingly endless string of cattle cars, blew its whistle as it rolled into the portal. In the distance blackish-gray smoke billowed furiously into the air from cigar-shaped spires, defiling the blue sky and the air with a horrendous and indefinable odor. My stomach churned with nausea.

"What in God's name is that horrible stench?" I asked as I covered my nose.

"You make me sick!" Veronika spat. "Don't toy with me. You know damn well what it is."

Birkenau had now faded into the distance behind us as we cruised on an open road with nothing but flat grassy fields sprinkled with a variety of trees. I removed my hand from my nose.

Fritz turned his head around. "Coast is clear, Jack."

I nodded and looked at Veronika. "I truly have no idea what's going on in those camps, Veronika."

Her eyes pinched with curiosity. "Why is he calling you Jack? Isn't your real name Adolf or some other flawless Aryan name?" As I chuckled she added, "And since when does a mere storm trooper call a big shot *SS Oberführer* by his first name?"

Just then Fritz joined my chuckle, which quickly escalated into a full-blown guffaw. I had to let her figure this out for herself, and as sure as sugar, my sweet, darling little Soviet, Italian, Jewish princess took a moment or two before saying, "No. This can't be. You're *really* Jack Goodwin? Are you kidding me, or is this some cruel Nazi mind game?"

Having finally simmered down, I grasped her hands and unlocked her shackles. "I'm sorry for speaking to you the way I did at the camp, but I had to play the role." I leaned over and kissed her on the forehead. "I'm so glad I found you. I'm just sorry it took this long." Tears welled in our eyes as she pulled me in for a heartfelt hug. "And I'm so glad you're the Jack Goodwin I first met. I knew you were my guardian angel." As we separated, she chuckled and covered her mouth. Removing her hand, she said, "Oh my! You apologized for how you spoke ill to me, yet I had said I wished you were dead. Dear God, please forgive me."

"Well, while you meant it at that time, I found it hard not to start laughing."

"But hold on a minute!" Veronika exclaimed as if her brain were jump-started with battery cables. "How did you ever manage to escape Hans Schmidt's torture chamber?"

Fritz looked in the rearview mirror at us. "Oh, this is a good one," he said in English.

"Yes," I said, "it is. But remember, Fritz, our lives depend upon complete immersion into our roles. So no more English until we land on British soil, once our mission is completed."

Fritz nodded as Veronika interjected in German, "Come on! I can't wait to hear this."

"Very well," I said. "As you'll recall, I was tied to a chair when you were dragged away by those goons." As she nodded, I continued, "And I played upon Hans's psyche for him to be a man and have our little session *mano e mano*."

"He agreed to that?"

"Not entirely, of course. He kept me tied, but dismissed his two thugs. Hans then attempted to scare the dickens out of me by pulling out his hedge shears."

"Dear God!" Veronika gasped.

"Well, he then attempted to frazzle me with his morbid little monologue. Which, come to think of it, I'll bet the bastard pilfered that passage from Edgar Allan Poe!" As Fritz laughed, and Veronika rolled her eyes, I continued,

"But then Hans approached me, snapping the shears to heighten the grisly drama. As he bent over to snip open my shirt, I *sprang up*. My chair and I lifted off the ground as my head smashed into his face, breaking his nose. As Hans fell backward to the floor, I hobbled my way over, hopping on the chair. On my last hop, I pushed hard, sailing into the air above his head. Gravity did the rest, as I came crashing down on his neck, crushing his larynx, while the spindle legs suitably pinned his dead carcass to the floor."

"Oh my God!" Veronika exclaimed. "That's incredible."

"Well, I had told you not to worry that day, and I also told Hans he'd regret it if he messed with me. After all, I take no shit from Schmidt!"

The three of us chuckled as we drove toward Munich into the setting sun.

St. Louis, Missouri
September 20, 1957

"Wow!" Eleanor exclaimed, "that *was* incredible. So, I guess you were Mom's knight in shining armor and proved Bronislaw wrong."

I smiled. "I suppose so, because I certainly wasn't Beatrice to guide her from Purgatory to Paradise."

Eleanor chuckled as she rose from the sofa and walked into the kitchen. She opened the refrigerator and pulled out a jar of Welch's grape jelly, Philadelphia cream cheese, and a bottle of milk. She turned to look at me. "Would you like me to make you a cream cheese and jelly sandwich?"

"No thanks, honey. I'll make myself some Chef Boyardee raviolis later."

Eleanor cringed. "Yuk! How can you eat that stuff? Its disgusting."

"Now, now, Ellie. I'll have you know that the founder, Ettore Boiardi, supplied the American troops through World War II, and even received a Gold Star after the war for his service. So that *stuff* kept many soldiers alive, including myself."

She gathered her milk and plate with two sandwiches and returned to the couch. "I can't believe how horrible a life Mom had. The things she saw and experienced are mindboggling. Auschwitz was horrifying."

"Indeed it was. Your mother and I had a discussion about that during our car ride."

Taking a bite of her sandwich, she said with food in her mouth, "Well...come on! Let's hear...about your ride...to Munich."

"First of all, don't talk with food in your mouth. Talk about gross!"

She chuckled and teasingly stuck out her tongue to show me the gooey mixture of slimy jelly, pasty cheese, and salivary bread.

I shook my head but chuckled. "You're a defiant gal, Ellie. And I like that. You need to learn to do what you believe in, not what others tell you. But that's *only if* your belief system is correct. Then let no one get in your way."

Her silly adolescent smile morphed into a pensive stiff upper lip. My daughter was getting to be a young woman and it was time for me to really start grooming her mind. Rather than long boring lectures or asking her to write impractical dissertations like the mandatory certificate factory does, I preferred another methodology. Basically, I've always believed a kernel of wisdom a day to cleanse the mind of the rubbish society injects into it was akin to adding a grain of chlorine a day into a large reservoir of polluted water—after a few years, the water will be purified.

Eleanor then responded, "But how can you ever truly know if your belief system is correct? Truth to one person is a falsehood to another. Millions of people believe Jesus is the Son of God, yet millions of Jews not only think he's a fake, but their ancestors made sure he was crucified."

That was another problem in trying to cleanse a child's mind, namely, when they throw your logic into a tailspin by presenting a brilliant rebuttal.

I glanced at the crude crayon drawing of the Crucifixion hanging on the wall. Ellie had drawn it when she was in Catechism a few years back, and despite its archaic technique, it oddly captured the ancient torture, which despite the school-taught notion that the Romans were the demons that invented crucifixion, the reality was that the savage Persians, Carthaginians, and Macedonians had nailed victims to a stake eons before. Meanwhile, the innocent Jews, of which Jesus was still a member, had only used stoning, strangulation, burning, and decapitation as humane methods to deal with blasphemy. The fact was that Rome was the height of civilization at that time, and the real barbarians were outside their borders. So deciphering truth from a treacherous past, filled with regimes and religions maligned by propaganda, and with false heroes and framed heretics, was a labyrinth best left to those in a prison cell or an insane asylum who had a lifetime to sort it all out.

"Well, honey, that is very true. That is why one must dig deep to unravel the *real* truth from many truths."

As Eleanor's face crinkled, trying to unravel that *truly* mystifying concept, I quickly switched gears and resumed our original tract. "Now getting back to Munich—" I leaned forward and looked her straight in the eye. "The journey from Auschwitz to Munich was only about an eight-hour car ride, but we had taken a long detour, stopping in Vienna, Austria for two days, to investigate the rumors that the Nazis had stolen countless works of art from the commandeered homes of rich Jews, which they had, and we then drove down into Italy."

"What pieces of artwork did they steal?"

"Many pieces, but the most prominent piece was perhaps the *Portrait of Adele Bloch-Bauer* or *Woman in Gold* by Gustav Klimt. Klimt was just one of many artists and composers who were tagged as degenerates by the Nazis, being that their work was too modern or that the creator was simply a Jew. So the Austrians easily managed to finagle possession of that avant-garde piece, yet the Nazis did confiscate many traditional paintings. Anyhow, we then traveled into Italy to visit your mother's hometown for several more days."

"Where was that?" Eleanor queried with bright eyes.

"A town called Azzano. It's a small but extremely beautiful location overlooking Lake Como. After the Hell and Purgatory your mother endured, Azzano was the closest thing I could take her to that resembled Paradise."

"Ah, so you *did* act like Beatrice after all," Eleanor opined.

I smiled. "I suppose so, but I'm just not as beautiful. Dante would never have been smitten by *me*, even from afar."

As Eleanor chuckled, I continued, "As much as Azzano was like Paradise, little did we know then, but three years later, Benito Mussolini would be assassinated a mere mile and a half away from your mother's birthplace. But as we both had discovered during those war years, there is no eternal Paradise on Earth, only the fleeting beautiful moments that wise people hold onto and cherish as precious memories."

"I guess that's sort of true," Eleanor said as she took a sip of milk. "You and Mom lived through some terrible times, and some great times."

"That's right, pumpkin, like when we had *you*." As Eleanor smiled, I continued, "Because you're a part of this convoluted story too. But first, we need to get back to my journey to Munich with your mother and Fritz. Fritz, by the way, was my OSS contact in Munich. His real name was Billy Coggan. After I had given Hans Schmidt a crushing demonstration of my lethal capabilities, I then smashed my-constrained-self into the cellar wall until the chair broke. Once I had untangled myself, I stole Hans's staff car and drove to Munich, where I rendezvoused with Billy, or rather, Fritz. As we had planned in London three months previously, I had flown into Poland with civilian clothing and Fritz had my new identity and SS uniform waiting for me. That's when Jack Goodwin became Johann Goldschmidt."

"Gold *Schmidt*?" Eleanor asked.

I nodded. "Yes, it was an odd coincidence how a part of my new name presaged the first man I had to kill to survive on that mission. But Goldschmidt I had become. However, quite fortunately, our mission was delayed, which aptly enabled my unscheduled rescue mission."

"To save Mom."

"Exactly!" I said as I lit up a Camel. Exhaling, I gazed into the smoky mist of my past, and paused for a moment. I then added, "Fritz wasn't thrilled about entering a concentration camp, but nothing would have prevented me from rescuing your mother. *Nothing*. God knows how she captured my heart then and still holds it today."

8

Alois Richter

July 28, 1942

*T*he horrid stench of Auschwitz was now far behind as Fritz floored the staff car and Veronika settled into the fact that I was indeed the Jack Goodwin she knew, and as I would soon find out—also loved. Yet as the trees whizzed by, along with my merry tale of escape from Hans Schmidt, Veronika's expression suddenly turned sour. I could see the pain of her hellish experiences written on her face as a wave of vengeful determination fueled her impassioned plea. "Jack, I'm elated that you saved me from that nightmare, but we *must* go back to save the rest of them."

"Listen, Veronika, although I now understand what the Nazis are truly doing in these camps my hands are tied. Orders are orders. That's the first and most important rule in this profession. Disobeying them costs lives, and quite possibly our lives too. I can offer that suggestion to my superiors, but they're the ones who will assess the situation and make all the strategic and logistical arrangements, *if* it's a sensible target."

"Sensible target!? Are you serious? Those demented Nazi pigs are systematically gassing and incinerating hundreds, no, thousands, of innocent men, women and children as if they were household garbage. It's pure insanity! How could anyone not do something to stop that immediately?"

"Veronika, I didn't mean sensible in that the mission is of little or no concern. What you've told me warrants serious attention. But—"

"But what?" Veronika snapped. "You managed to perform an unscheduled rescue mission for *me*, so why not rescue thousands of others? Not to mention punishing psychopathic criminals like Bronislaw Sinkowski."

"It's not that simple. It took me months just to plan your single rescue mission, and I was only allotted that time because my main mission was delayed."

As Veronika's heated passion began to simmer, I continued, "And once you hear my mission, you'll understand that sometimes other missions take priority."

Fritz's eyes widened as he gazed at me in the rearview mirror. "Are you nuts!? You're not going to let her know our mission, are you?"

Meanwhile, Veronika simultaneously retorted, "Priority!? What could possibly take priority over a death camp?"

I momentarily ignored Fritz and responded, "Veronika, the toxic master of that evil camp is a Germanic germ called Adolf Hitler. And my current mission just so happens to entail heading to Munich, where Fritz and I will set into motion a well-thought-out plan to exterminate that Teutonic parasite. Then there will be no more Auschwitz. So, yes, one must set priorities during a war."

Fritz and Veronika both choked in astonishment. Having pissed off Fritz and tamed Veronika, I instructed Fritz to slow down and begin our long detour.

Having stayed first in Austria and then settling in Italy, it was clear to Fritz that he was the dreaded third wheel. Nevertheless, we always tried to include him in our activities—well, most activities. Veronika and I had fallen deeply in love. And those four days in Lake Como were magical. Whether it was pure chemistry or the horrors of war that drew us together, I'm not sure, but we bonded— physically, numerous times—thus planting the seed of our eventual marriage; we would be parents in nine months.

Finally arriving in Munich, Fritz and Veronika had to lie low in a safe house while I began parading around Munich as *SS Oberführer* Johann Goldschmidt. My mission, the most dangerous and difficult task ever contemplated, had been attempted at least twenty-four times between 1921 and 1942—all unsuccessful. Either Hitler was a predestined demigod protected by Lucifer to rule Earth, or his Gestapo grunts were the most loyal and efficient bloodhounds to ever roam the planet, because the madman was seemingly untouchable.

That is why we had no illusions about Operation Phantom—even though a phantom *is* an illusion. I don't know whom the genius was that came up with the code name of our mission, but I would have much preferred a name like Operation Dead Dog, something positive to really motivate us. Anyhow, we all knew how elusive our target was and how perilous it was to even attempt an assassination, as the tales of a few of our brazen predecessors were burned into our minds to remind us of the many failures.

Georg Elser had tried to assassinate Hitler back on November 8, 1939. Having worked at the Waldenmaier armament factory in Heidenheim and later at the Vollmer quarry in Königsbronn, Elser managed to pilfer explosives and detonators. Although in harmony with Nazism, Elser grew disenchanted with Hitler, Goebbels, and Goering—the unholy trinity of the ungodly Third Reich. Knowing that Hitler celebrated his famous Beer Hall Putsch annually at the *Bürgerbräukeller* in Munich, Elser surveilled the hall the previous year. He determined that the optimal location for his explosive would be in the pillar directly behind the podium where Hitler habitually ignited his audiences with his well-choreographed diatribes.

Having gained access to the hall at night, Elser worked on notching out the pillar and installing his time bomb over the course of two months. With everything set to go, literally at 9:20 P.M., Elser waited impatiently for Hitler to arrive and give his long-winded oration. However, that evening Hitler cut his speech short, leaving the building at 9:07. Within those thirteen minutes Hitler was already on his way to Nuremburg when the bomb exploded. Seven people were killed instantly and sixty-three injured when the pillar exploded and parts of the building collapsed. Elser was later caught and now sits in Dachau prison awaiting a grim fate.

As we at the OSS learned later on, Hitler was not only relieved to have left early and avoided death, but worse yet, he now believed that Providence had looked over him and ordained his glorious mission, thus goading the almighty *Führer* to reach his goal. And that Hitler miraculously evaded death some twenty-four times; I was beginning to believe it myself!

The only small consolation I have is that Hitler's sentimental *Bürgerbräu* soapbox was reduced to rubble and never rebuilt. But being as intrepid as his *Blitzkrieg*, Hitler relocated his annual commemorations to the *Löwenbräukeller* at *Stiglmaierplatz* right in Munich. With that in mind, my mission now was to reconnoiter the *Löwenbräukeller*.

Dressed in my ominous, black *SS Oberführer* uniform, with its Sam Browne belt with holster and service dagger, red arm band with swastika, twin oak leaves on the collar patches, and my sinister cap with a silver Death's Head insignia, I now strolled toward the *Löwenbräukeller* with my new bride. It was against my better judgment, but Veronika wanted to be a part of the mission, and I conceded. Naturally Fritz was not thrilled about this unauthorized secret arrangement and reminded me of my own words "orders are orders," but rules were meant to be broken, especially when a gorgeous woman—who also happened to be carrying my baby—was involved.

As we approached this historic edifice, with its round tower with pilasters, a coned-shaped roof and aptly decorated with the Löwenbräu lion, it was clear to see why Hitler chose this venue. The WWI corporal, who had twice failed to gain entry into the art academy, never held a real job, and who had lived in poverty, moved up in the world. Veronika and I strolled inside and peered into the dining room, and then headed toward the grand hall. As I looked at this spacious room, with its two-storied wooden ceiling and series of soft curving arches on the floor level and upper tier, my mind searched for the optimal location to plant our bomb.

Veronika knew my intentions and could see my surveilling eyes in motion as she whispered, "How could you blow up such a nice building?"

My eyes darted towards her electric light-blue irises. "Sacrifices must be made. Remember, *priorities.*"

As we walked into the crowd of inebriated citizens, soldiers and several officers, each trying to escape the war for an hour or many hours, a roaming waiter handed me two *krugs* of beer.

"*Danke,*" I said, "How much will that be?"

The elderly man gazed at me with a nervous smile. "For you, *Oberführer,* and your lovely lady, no charge."

Before I could even respond, the waiter scurried off. It was clear to see that even here in Bavaria the townsfolk were wary of being snagged by the Gestapo or SS for some convoluted charge of treason or simply having found a distant relative of theirs who might have an ounce of Jewish blood. The reality of that insanity really hit home with Veronika's incident, whose mother had even converted to Catholicism, yet Veronika, who was raised Catholic, was still deemed a half Jew. So by Nazi logic, a person's bloodline is not so much dictated by ethnicity but more so by their religion—even if they abandon it for another. It's clear to see that the Germans' bigoted brainstorm is simply a buffoonish blunder by a bloodthirsty bunch of brainless baboons. Son of a B that was a lot of Bs.

After handing Veronika her beer, I then took a swig of the tasty Lion's brew. No sooner had the creamy liquid slid down my gullet, than out of the corner of my eye I spotted this handsome *Oberführer* eyeing up my bride. Worse yet, the Nazi pig was walking right toward us, or rather toward Veronika. Stopping before us, he said to me while looking at Veronika, "*Willkommen* to Munich, *Oberführer*."

"Are you sure it's *me* that you are welcoming?" I retorted.

The Aryan Adonis with magnetic blue eyes, dark hair, and perfectly chiseled features, laughed as he finally turned to notice whom he was talking to. "Well, yes, I welcome you both. I have not seen either of you here before. What are your names?"

I already hated this nosy, pompous prick. Slapping on my pseudo smile, I replied, "I am *Oberführer* Johann Goldschmidt," and the part I loved saying, "and this is *my wife*, Veronika Goldschmidt."

As I glanced at Veronika, my gloating smile withered. It was clear that my demented wife truly enjoyed the intrusion by this phony, obnoxious moron. As their eyes reconnected, I interrupted, "And what is *your* name, *Oberführer*?"

The handsome lounge lizard, towering at six-feet-four-inches tall, merely glanced down at me—as if annoyed by *my* imposition—and replied, "Richter, Alois Richter."

With his charming smile, the lizard asked Veronika, "So, how long have you been married?"

Now this rogue's brass really burned my ass as I interrupted again, "Why does it matter? Whether it's a day or a decade, she's *my* wife, *Oberführer* Reptile."

Veronika's giddy smile quickly deflated while Alois the Aryan Adonis finally turned completely in my direction. "The name is *Richter*. Please, do not take my friendly curiosity as being dishonorable, *Oberführer* Goldschmidt. I am simply glad to have a fellow *Oberführer* stationed here in Munich."

Again, I slapped on my pseudo smile for this charismatic reptile, and replied, "Well, we might be leaving Munich soon, very soon. And—"

"No we're not," Veronika chimed in, ruining my exit strategy. "You said you were stationed here for several weeks, Johann."

My eyes rolled toward my babbling bride. "Yes, my dear, but I just received word an hour ago that I may be needed in Dresden. I apologize, it slipped my mind."

"Well," Alois interjected, "'*may be needed*' does not sound too definite to me."

One thing was *definite*: I loathed this son of a SS snake!

"Please," he said, "join me for a splendid meal in the dining room. The chefs here cater to us SS officers as if we were kings."

And I wish Alois were King Charles I of England as I'd gladly volunteer to behead the treasonous fop!

Veronika, however, jumped at the invitation like a daffy show dog doing back flips through a hoop. "That would be splendid! Thank you, *Oberführer* Richter." Turning toward me, she added, "Isn't that delightful?"

More like devious, but I nodded. "Yes, of course, how gracious of you, *Oberführer* Reptile, I mean Richter."

Alois rolled his eyes. "Please" he said, "we are of the same rank, and I hope to become good friends, so dispense with the hostility and formalities. Just call me Alois."

I'd rather call him A-louse, but I nodded cordially. "Of course," I said, as I slapped him on the back *heartily*. "Alois it is! I hope they make good sauerkraut?" Because I'd enjoy nothing more than chewing up this sour Kraut and spitting him out.

Alois looked at me and swung his arm around my shoulders. With his gorgeous smile, revealing his perfect set of canines, the suave wolf simply chuckled and escorted me toward the dining room while grasping my lovely sheep's hand to follow. Meanwhile, Veronika, the loopy lamb, beamed with delight.

Granted, Veronika had been through hell at Auschwitz and had not been treated kindly, nor had she eaten well, so I could understand her enthusiasm, especially since our new host was damn good looking to boot. But there was something off about this Kraut, something that the little voice in my head kept saying "Give this Kraut *das boot!*"

As we entered the dining room Alois was warmly greeted as the maître d' fawned all over him like royalty. Showing us to our table, Sir Maître d' Kiss-Ass pulled out our chairs and rattled off the menu. Alois ordered for us, as if we were children, yet his gesture was clearly twofold: first, to entreat us to the special dishes *he* wanted us to taste, and second, because he wanted to treat us like children! It was that damned alpha thing that grated on my nerves—at least when it wasn't me being the alpha.

I wish I could say that was the only evening I had to suffer with Alois the louse, but it wasn't. Two months passed and the three of us became entangled in a proverbial love triangle. Actually, I wish Alois would have gotten lost in the Bermuda Triangle, but fate mocked me. And it wasn't that Alois and Veronika had sexual relations, but the gleam in this snake's eyes when he gazed at her could not be mistaken for anything else but envy and lust. Being a trained OSS agent, I had a knack for picking up on telltale signs, and if Alois kept it up much longer, he would have to make the sign—the Sign of the Cross—before I pummeled his perfect, pretty face, ramming his sparkling Chiclets down his throat!

It wasn't that I'm a jealous guy—okay, scrap that. I *am* a jealous guy—and this *Vaffen* vermin was getting under my skin, like a bloodthirsty tick. We frequented several beer cellars over the past two months but the *Löwenbräukeller* had become our main stomping ground. And while Operation Phantom was delayed once again, this time due to concerns I raised about the tightened security, Operation Veronika seemed to be in full swing for Alois.

Once again at our haunt, Veronika, as usual, was sitting across from Alois as we downed some frothy ale and chomped on some pretzels. Their conversation centered on music, being that Mr. Perfect was also a professional violinist for the Weimar Philharmonic. Alois bragged about knowing the composer Richard Strauss and some Italian composer named Alfredo Casella, since Alois's mother was Italian. I guess that's what allowed the Aryan to even consider listening to non-German composers. Anyhow, he went on and on about Casella's *Second Symphony*, which he hailed as being a neglected masterpiece that was even greater than Gustav Mahler's *Second Symphony*. While some people claimed Casella copied aspects of Mahler's *Second Symphony*, Alois told Veronika Casella's symphony was actually completed *before* Mahler's, which negated the criticisms. Moreover, Casella's symphony launched with the most emotional funeral dirge he'd ever heard with soft, eerie strings and tolling bells which then morphed into an ominous military march. He said it perfectly captured the essence of war and death.

They talked for hours, especially since they shared some Italian blood and Veronika's dad was in the music field so they knew a lot of the same people. Naturally, that further cemented their bond as their intense conversation and souls seemed to intertwine like an intoxicating grapevine fugue. Their cultural conversation, however, shifted from symphonic chatter to a very serious matter as Alois unexpectedly broke off his bragging banter with my wife and bludgeoned me with, "So, Johann, Veronika had mentioned that you were originally stationed here to make an inspection of the Auschwitz camp." Wiping the beer foam off his wily mouth, he added, "So, how did that go? And what did you think of Commandant Höss?"

I felt like I was smacked from the *Löwenbräukeller* into the *Auto-da-fé*, as the Nazi inquisitor gazed at me with his frigid blue eyes. Perhaps it was the twelve beers or the fact that the whole conversation that night had excluded me, but I was off. Even my well-trained poker face was off duty as I sat mute with my eyes dilated, not from alcohol but clearly from surprise. Basically, I looked like a stunned tarsier.

Veronika jumped in, but not the way I had coached her. "It didn't go very well, actually. Johann informed me that Commandant Höss runs a barbaric operation there. One that demands serious attention."

My jaw dropped. *Shit! Why did I bring her into this dangerous operation? What the hell was I thinking? Oh, yes, perhaps it was more than my brain that was thinking, but Christ, she just opened a can of worms—deadly Nazi bloodsucking worms!*

I shook my head, hoping it would whisk away the alcohol in my head and clear my thoughts, because some fancy footwork was needed—and *fast*.

But Alois responded quickly, his eyes wide with curiosity. "Barbaric? Just what is Höss doing there? And what sort of attention?"

There he went again. Alois could never ask one question; it was always an MG 42 open-bolt machine gun bulleting me with a barrage of questions. Now shell shocked, I blinked hard as Veronika jumped back into the fray. "Alois, when prisoners enter Auschwitz, some are culled for hard labor but the majority drift up the chimney or become silt at the bottom of the Vistula River." As Alois and I squinted, confused, she heatedly continued, "Höss has setup an elaborate extermination facility of diabolical proportions. And German efficiency is utilizing every inch of these prisoners, from their shoes and clothes—that will keep Germans warm—to their jewelry and gold teeth—that will fund the Reich—to the hair on their heads—that was cut off and used to stuff pillows and mattresses so Aryans can get a good rest after a grueling day of mass murder. It's insane! And Höss completed Birkenau several months ago, so I shudder to think of how many Jews, gypsies, and undesirables he has gassed and cremated since then."

Richter's eyebrows rose as I turned flush. Heightening my surprise was Richter's response. "I'm glad you feel the same way," he whispered as he took a drag of his slim Muratti. "I have heard only rumors to that effect, but coming from you, Veronika, I now believe this tragedy is patent."

Taking another puff, he then turned toward me. "Your wife is right, Johann. We *must* do something about this!"

My head throbbed from the gears churning in my cerebral crankcase. *Was Alois just playing along, only to snag us both at the camp while allegedly rectifying Höss's sins? How convenient it would be to toss us both into the gas chamber and incinerate our bodies into a fine dust. What the hell was truly going on in this Nazi's fiendish head?*

"What exactly do you suggest?" My mouth uttered, now operating on autopilot.

Alois extinguished his girly cigarette and drew his chair in closer to the table. He then leaned forward, motioning us to bring ourselves into his secure huddle.

"I'm a savvy judge of character," he said, "and I had sensed from the moment we met that you both were honest Germans, with integrity and morals."

I laughed inside. Good judge my ass! Neither one of us was a crazy Kraut. Furthermore, my morals were being depleted rapidly in this damn war, especially since I'd been having recurring thoughts of committing a mortal sin by strangling this shifty-eyed jackal sitting before me.

Veronika nodded graciously. "Thank you, Alois. I feel the same way about you." Glancing at me with disappointment in her eyes, she continued, "I've been asking Johann to take action for months, but, alas, he has sat idle, like he is now."

Now my blood was *really* boiling! This had gone too far. Was this a *coup d'état* these two lovers worked up together? Okay, lovers may be a bit strong and premature, but Christ, Veronika is carrying my baby! How could she dis me like this?

Richter shook his inebriated head. "Don't blame your husband, Veronika," he said, his voice gaining volume. "This is a very delicate situation. Rudolf Höss is a long-time friend to Heinrich Himmler." Alois peered around the room briefly, and continued, "Those two morons were mere farmers, but are now judges and executioners who control the fates of millions of innocent people." Alois took another sip of beer, perhaps to bolster his courage to confess his treasonous thoughts or to better elaborate his treacherous lie.

I, on the other hand, pushed my *krug* away. I didn't need more alcohol to further cloud my already-full head of his beguiling bullshit. Could this Kraut truly be a German with a heart and soul, or was he just another devious wolf luring us into his lair to devour us? As I bit into a nice salty pretzel, he continued, "Furthermore, I'm enraged by Hitler's latest rhetoric that all foreign Jews must be exterminated. The world thinks it's idle chatter, but as we now know, it's not! The *Führer* and his evil henchmen are all mad. They *must* be brought down."

I sat mute, assessing what was going on inside this snake's head as Veronika replied, "Yes! I agree, Alois. We must!" Gazing at me, she whispered, "Alois and I have discussed many things in private that I guess I should have told you, but I know he is sincere and willing to help us."

I sprang up onto my feet, accidently hitting the table and knocking over my beer. As the amber liquid spread rapidly across the table and onto Richter's lap, I spat, "This conversation is over!" Leaning over the table, I whispered furiously, "You're both speaking treason. And that is why I've kept idle all these months." Taking a quick glance around the room I noticed several eyes had focused on my rousing actions. I looked at my wife. "Let's go!" I hissed through clenched teeth. "This man will get us all killed."

With that, I grabbed Veronika's hand and pulled her up. As I heatedly escorted my insane wife out the door, while she mumbled objections, I could hear the sound of boots hitting the pavement behind us. Sensing it was Richter and his Gestapo henchmen to arrest us, I stopped short and spun around. Alois almost collided into us, his face marred with regret as he uttered, "I apologize. Perhaps the Löwenbräu loosened my tongue too much. But what I spoke was from the heart. I know you're an OSS spy, Johann. And I want in."

I closed my eyes and then peered down at Veronika. "What lies have you been telling him?"

"No, lies," Veronika blurted, "just the truth. Alois had already confided in me that he despised Hitler and has ties with Henning von Tresckow."

My eyes darted toward Richter, who nodded his approval, and then surveilled the area. With no one near us, I shook my head. "I don't believe you, Alois." I knew darn well that Henning von Tresckow was a chief operations officer with strong political connections, who according to intelligence at OSS, was the leader of the German resistance, and had even tried to assassinate Hitler two years ago.

"You must believe me!" Alois pleaded. "Besides, I wouldn't have admitted it to you if I feared being brought in on charges of treason, now would I?"

"I don't know you well enough to trust anything you say, Alois. But evidently my wife does." My heated eyes glanced at Veronika, who interjected, "And just what do you think has been going on between Alois and I?"

"Evidently I don't know you well enough either," I spat. "All I know is that I'm sick of my pregnant wife spending time alone with this charming reptile!"

Richter fell silent as Veronika retorted, "Johann, you know darn well how much I love you. Your jealously is clouding your vision."

"Oh, I see clearly, my dear. It's you two that have clouded vision. First, you both speak of treason in a public beer hall. Second, you confess that you two have had private meetings. And finally you think I'm insane enough to join you on some crazy scheme to bring down one of Himmler's main camps."

Richter finally spoke up. "Listen, Johann, you have nothing to fear from us. We're all on the same side."

Nothing to fear from *us!* Now this snake in the grass was making *me* the outsider with my own wife. If that wasn't a confession of guilt I don't know what is.

"He's right, honey," Veronika interjected. "He may have been careless about speaking out tonight, but as he said, perhaps it was the beer talking."

"Oh, no!" I said, "It wasn't the Löwenbräu Lion who was speaking, it was Alois the Loose-Lipped Liability who was talking. And if he can't control his mouth with a few pints in him then he's not cut out to be a spy!"

Richter grasped my shoulder. "I just had a bad night, that's all," he retorted.

I removed his hand off my shoulder. "Don't touch me, Alois!" I barked. "One bad night is all you need to get yourself killed, and all those around you. Even if I were a spy, I would never team up with a guy like you. Are you clever enough to read me now, Alois?"

With a smirk, he nodded. "Yes, I forgot. Jack Goodwin is not an OSS spy, nor has he ever made a single mistake. Shit! You're flawless, Jack, save for you lack of judgment."

Alois flew backwards, hitting the ground, after my fist smashed him hard in the jaw!

Veronika knelt by his side as Richter held his bloody lip and said, "Okay, maybe I deserved that, but—"

"But nothing!" I barked, "If you ever speak those words again in an open public square, I *will* kill you! Do you understand me? So do us all a favor, stick to your violin!" I was about to walk away when I stopped. "Then again, I take that back. Knowing you, you'd end up being a Nazi Nero, fiddling away as the world burns from your stupidity!"

Luckily no one was in earshot of our altercation, but hell, I've been looking for an opportunity to belt this bastard in his big yappy mouth for months and chew him out. So I just had to seize the moment. And damn, it felt good!

Meanwhile my traitorous wife helped the drunk up to his feet as she shook her head at *me*. Somehow I was always the bad guy between these two. I didn't know how that happened, but worse yet, I was dumbfounded. How could I possibly change this mess around? I just wanted my wife back. Back to the days when we gazed into each other's eyes and didn't have to even speak a word, yet felt like the world was spinning on our command, our every heartbeat rotating the Earth as if a perfect Swiss clock, as each minute passed, sending us into an ethereal world of pure bliss and unbound passion. How I wished I could turn back that clock to those precious moments. But a Nazi wrench was tossed into our perfectly crafted instrument and was now breaking us apart, and breaking my heart. The pain hit me hard, harder than the punch that just sent Alois careening to the ground. He was the lucky one, already recovering from his pain. Yet somehow I knew mine would last days, months, or possibly a lifetime.

St. Louis, Missouri
September 20, 1957

Eleanor's eyes were glazed with tears. "Dad, you never told me about this sad love triangle. Was Mom unfaithful?"

I reached over to hand her a napkin. "Well, that's something I'll never know for sure, but I strongly doubt it. I believe it was more my jealousy than any possible indiscretion on her part."

Eleanor wiped her eyes as her face contorted into a vengeful smirk. "That Alois Richter was a no-good bastard! Now I can understand why you hate him so much."

"Well, hold onto that hatred, because the plot thickens, as will your loathing once you hear the rest of this chilling tale."

9

Death & Resurrection

October 2, 1942

*T*hat same night Veronika and I walked back to our apartment building with Alois trailing two steps behind. It certainly wasn't my idea to have the snake slither in our wake, but Veronika had begged me to give the reptile another chance.

As we stepped inside our flat, Fritz confronted us with a serious expression on his face. He gazed over my shoulder, spotting Alois. "Is everything all right?" he asked.

I glanced back at Richter, who was holding a handkerchief to his bloody lip, then back at Fritz. "Well, it's all right for *me*. What's up?"

Fritz hesitated, then whispered, "What's *he* doing here?"

Veronika rolled her eyes. "It's fine," she said loudly. "Alois is one of us. He wants to join the OSS as a double agent."

Fritz' eyes widened, as I interjected, "Now hold on, Veronika! You're in no position to act as both his lawyer and recruiting officer."

As she was about to rip into me with a fiery retort, Fritz cut in, "But is it true?"

Before I could respond, Alois and Veronika spoke in unison, eerily as if it were rehearsed. "Yes! It's true."

Now it was time for *me* to roll *my* eyes. "That's what *they* claim, Fritz. But Alois has not been vetted." Clutching my Luger, I pointed it at Richter's head. "Now sit down and tell me everything you know about Henning von Tresckow." I quickly looked at my wife and barked, "And *you* shut up!"

The look on my face was clearly enough for any sane person to comply and, happily, my wife showed that she wasn't totally insane for falling in with this *brat*, who was the *wurst* German piece of pork I'd ever come across.

Richter obliged by not only sitting, but also expounding upon a wealth of valuable information, mentioning how General Friedrich Olbricht, the planner of Operation Valkyrie, was communicating with Henning von Tresckow regarding a major coup d'état. Richter also mentioned other names, dates, and plots, one being set to occur in two days, thus clearly easing me into a believer—well, actually a quasi-believer.

"Very well, Alois," I said. "You made a solid case for being legit. But I'm skeptical by nature. So you're not going to leave my sight until this latest plot you mentioned truly materializes in two days."

"You can't hold him at gun point," my dear wife interjected adamantly.

"I certainly can and *will!*" I barked. "And if there's no sign of sabotage at the oil refinery in Mannheim, like he mentioned, Alois just might find a bullet in his head!"

Fritz suddenly jumped into the mounting storm. "Jack, you can't hold him here for two days," he gushed in English.

My eyes heatedly darted back to Fritz. "What did I say about calling me by that name, and in English?"

"I'm s-sorry," Fritz fumbled, "but I was meaning to tell you when you arrived that I received word that you—Oh dear! Should I continue?" He glanced at Alois.

I shook my head. "Christ almighty! I'm surrounded by assassins. *None* of you can be trusted."

As Fritz cowered, I lowered my Luger to my side. "Go on, we're all in this mess together now."

Fritz sheepishly looked up at me. "I received instructions from London. You see, they forced it out of me."

"Forced what out of you?" I commanded.

"Well, they had pressured me numerous times, asking where you had been many nights, and, well, I sort of told them that you were with Veronika, your wife."

"You *what!*"

Fritz shuddered as his frantic eyes darted at Veronika and back at me. "Well, they kept hounding me, and I...I ran out of lies, so I told them the truth."

I shook my head. "This is a bad dream. So how much truth did they suck out of your tightly stitched lips?"

Fritz smirked as he replied, "That she's a Soviet air pilot that defected and is now pregnant and willing to aid our efforts."

"Good God!" I blurted. "They'll have my head."

"Not exactly," Fritz said with assurance. "Actually, they were very understanding."

"Well, I'm glad *they* are, because *I'm* not!"

"Simmer down," Veronika interjected. "Let him speak. It sounds like you're making a mountain out of a mole hill."

My eyes rolled. "I'd like to make a mountain rather than a mole hill on his blabbering head!"

"Calm that bad Irish temper of yours!" she shouted.

I laughed. "Look who's yelling—the zesty Italian Night Witch."

Alois sat mute, just watching the fireworks, while Fritz chimed in to douse the flames. "Listen to me! Headquarters has no reprimands in line, as far as I know. They just want you to take Veronika to Hamburg tonight."

"Hamburg? Tonight!?" Veronika and I responded, confused.

"Yes, Hamburg. From there you'll meet a contact that will put her on a ship to London." He glanced at my bewildered wife. "Now that they know you are married and with child, Veronika, they want to keep you both out of harm's way."

"Oh swell!" I said with a chuckle. "The bombed city of London, where the *Luftwaffe* dropped bombs and citizens live like rats in the Tubes."

Alois suddenly awakened. "Well, better to be hit by enemy fire there than friendly fire here."

Again I chuckled. "Does *how* one die really matter? One way or another you're dead!"

"If it doesn't matter to you," he replied, "then you should get her to Hamburg and on that boat to London."

"Listen up, chump! I said *how* one dies doesn't really matter. But putting yourself from one war zone into another is by no means *out of harm's way!* And where do *you* come off thinking you even have a say in my wife's affairs? Shut the fuck up!"

Angrily, Alois sprang up with fists drawn and his face twisted as Veronika stepped over and gently eased him back into his seat. "Never mind you two deciding my fate. I'll be the one who decides where I'll go. And I opt for going to London. It *is* safer, and I must think of the baby."

Alois's face mellowed with relief, while mine twisted with grief. "So, you opt for Alois's wishes, not mine?"

"Stop being so damn petulant!" she barked. "We'll soon have our own cranky little child to pacify. I don't need two babies."

As Fritz and Alois laughed I heatedly rolled my eyes. And with these three clowns I seem to be rolling my eyes far more than usual.

Having won the argument, Veronika prodded me to prepare for our flight to Hamburg. In a last ditch effort to be with his unrequited love, Alois begged to prove his loyalty by tagging along. His plea to make an appeal to OSS contacts in either Hamburg or London was sound, yet being the petulant jealous baby that I was, I flat out rejected his idea of settling his untrustworthy ass in London near my beautiful wife.

That night, on October 2, 1942, we set off on our notorious flight in the Junkers Ju 52, which I had already described in vivid detail. However, what I hadn't mentioned was how that struggle began.

As we three sat in the mostly barren fuselage with the pilot and navigator, Alois and I engaged in one of those alpha male debates, which naturally centered on my wife, and quickly escalated into a full-blown brawl. It pains me to recall how that filthy Kraut won the upper hand that night, but out the plane I went as the prick pushed me to my intended death. Fortunately for me, a bit of Hitler's luck stepped in and I managed to deploy the parachute that I had clutched seconds before Richter's malicious body toss.

Having landed safely, and only several miles west of Hamburg, I made my way into the city by late afternoon. My SS uniform was torn and I was missing my cherished Death Skull officer's cap. Citizens turned to gape, but quickly veered away, thanks to my rank and the utter fear that I had